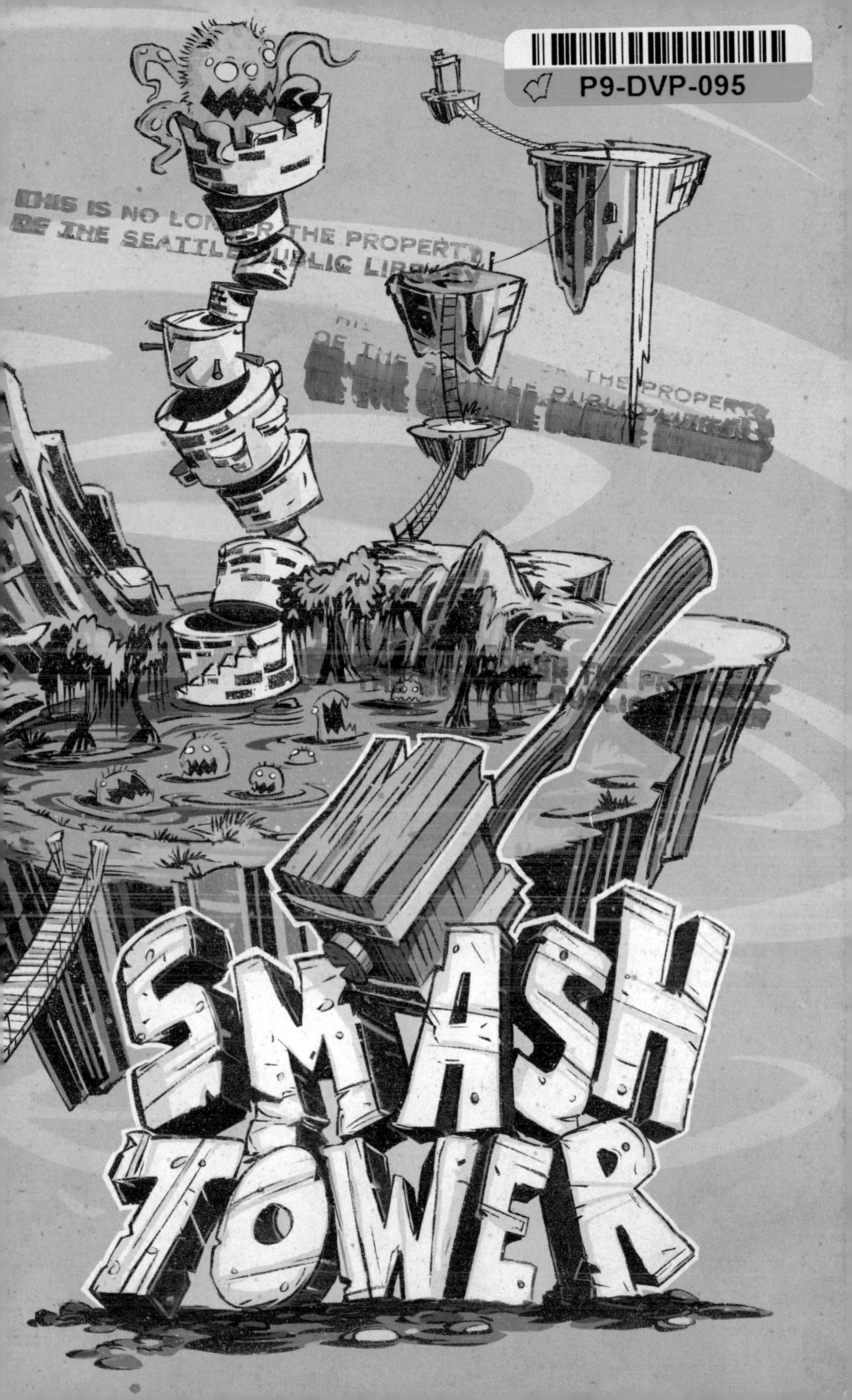
SMASH
TOWER

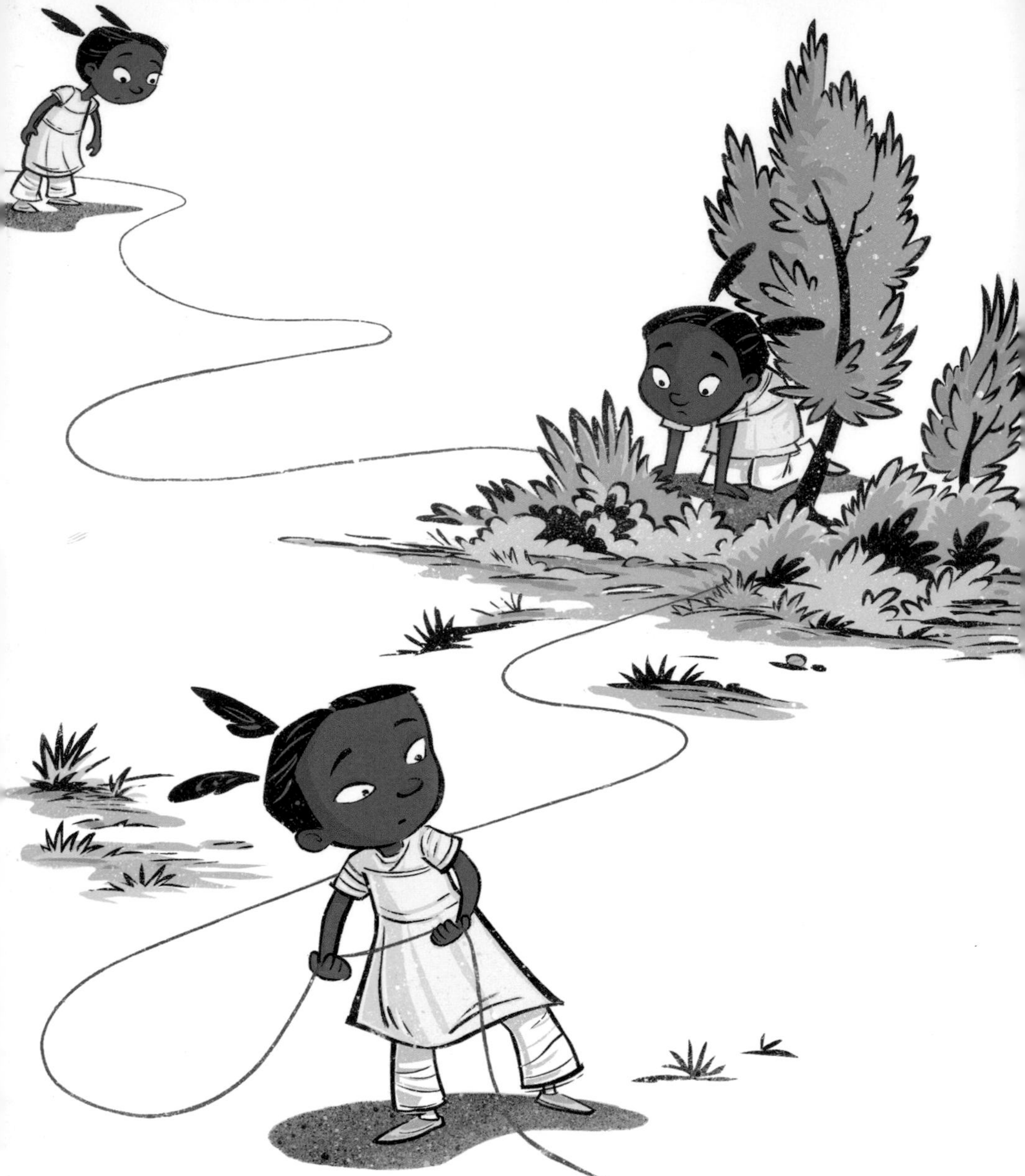

I'M OGRE IT

Jeffrey Ebbeler

I Like to Read® COMICS™

HOLIDAY HOUSE · NEW YORK

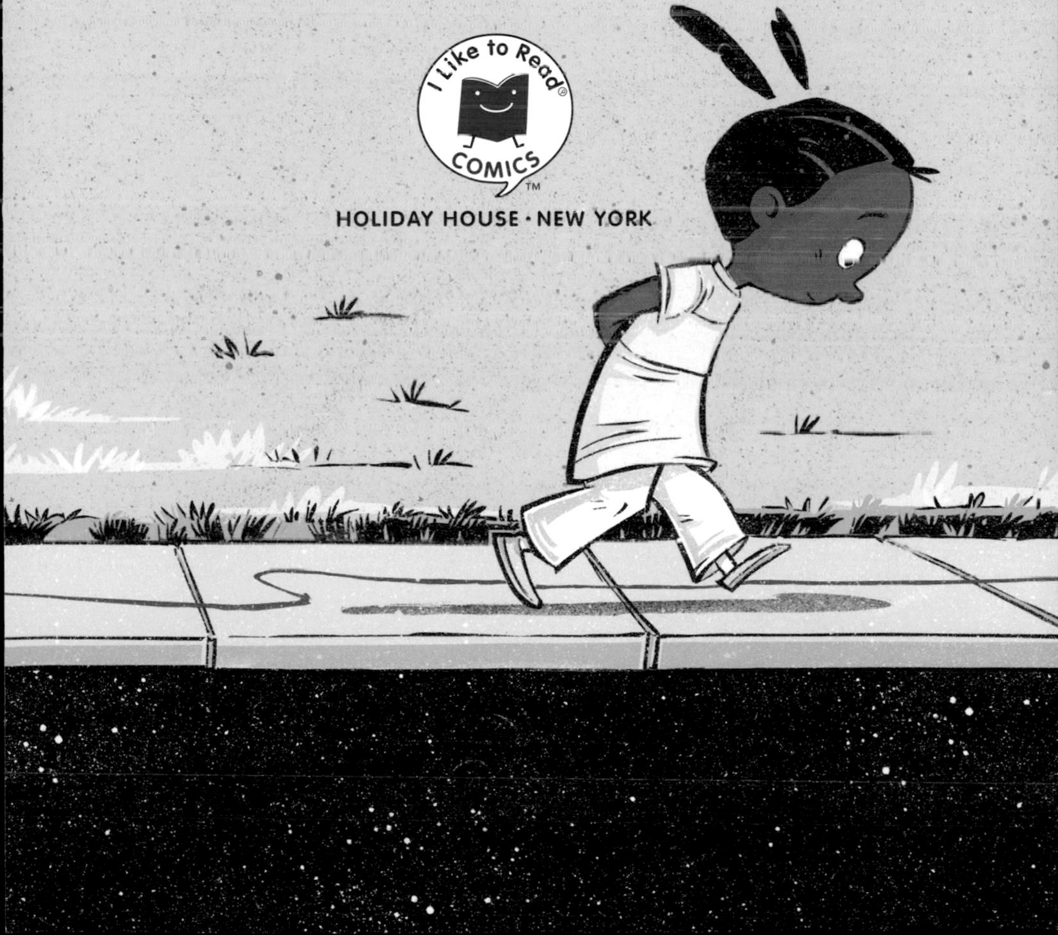

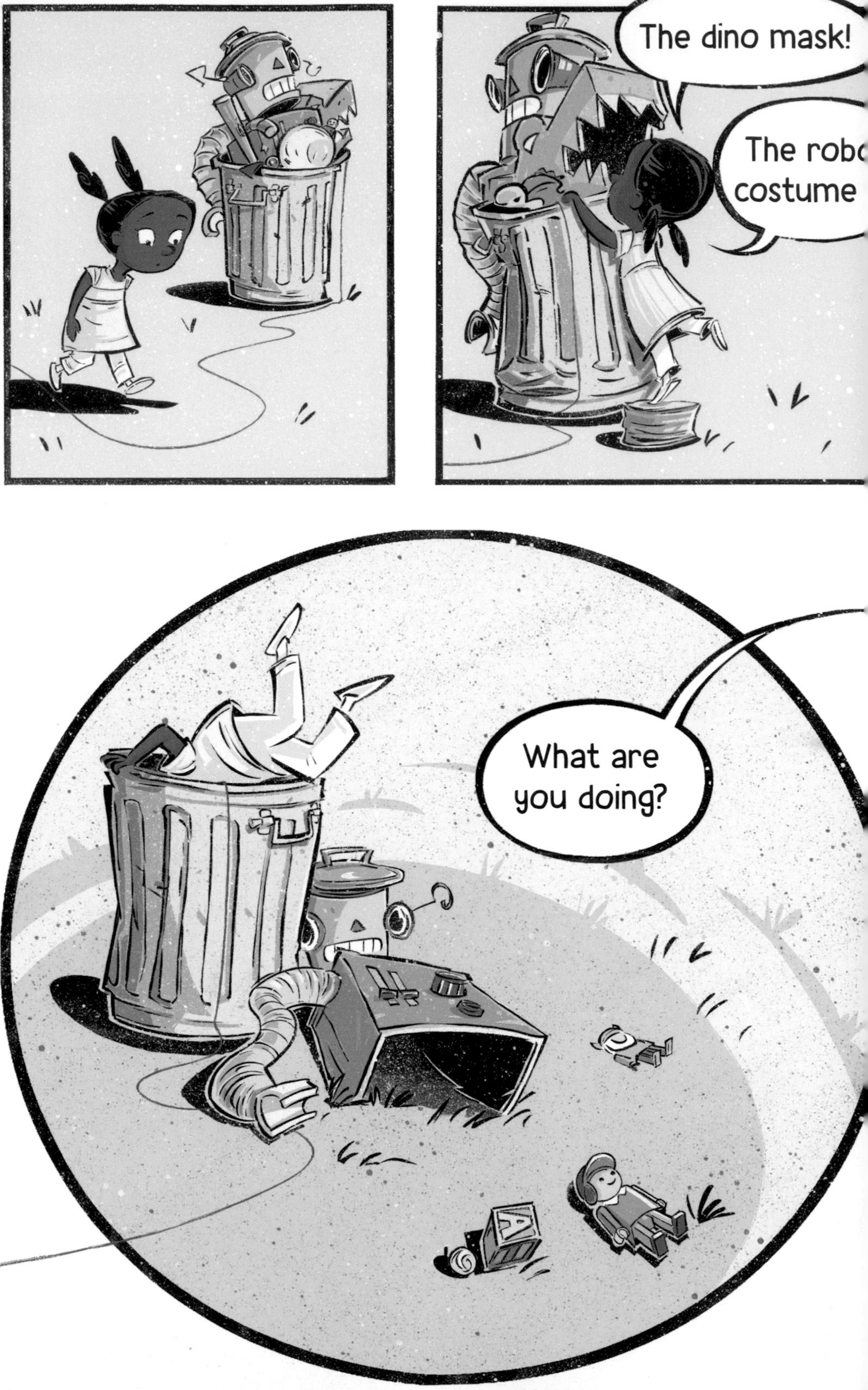
The dino mask!
The rob
costume
What are you doing?

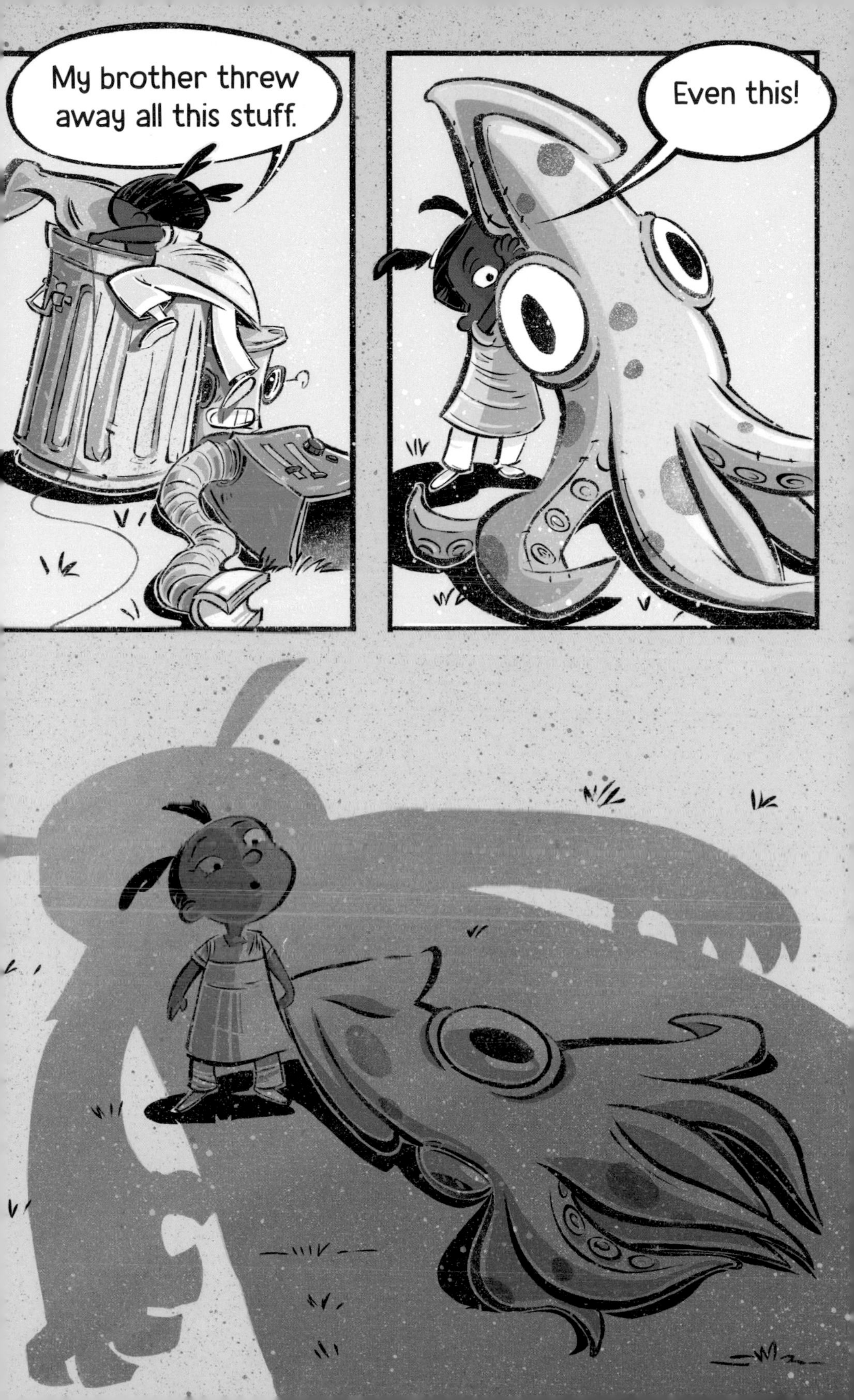
My brother threw away all this stuff.
Even this!

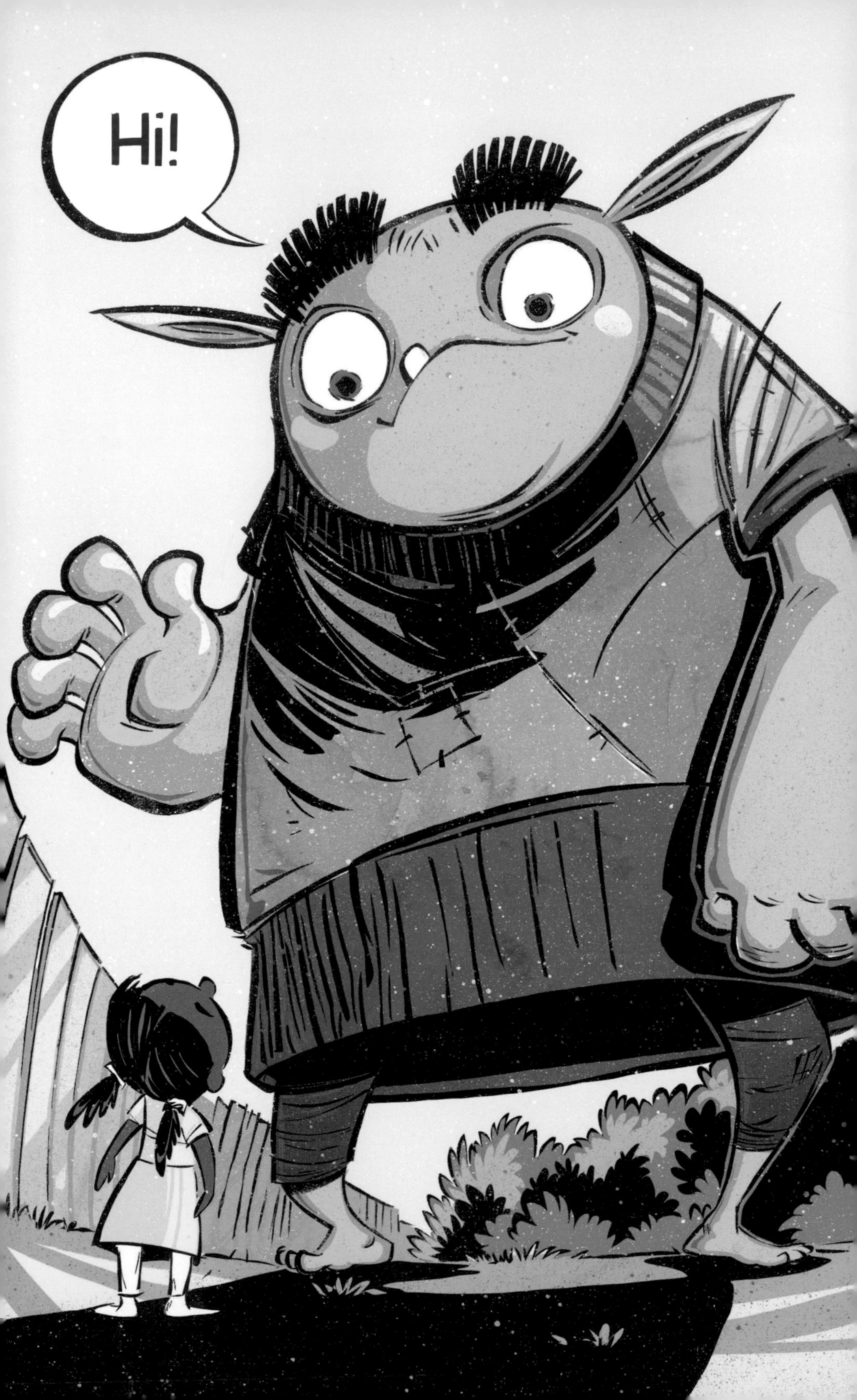
Hi!

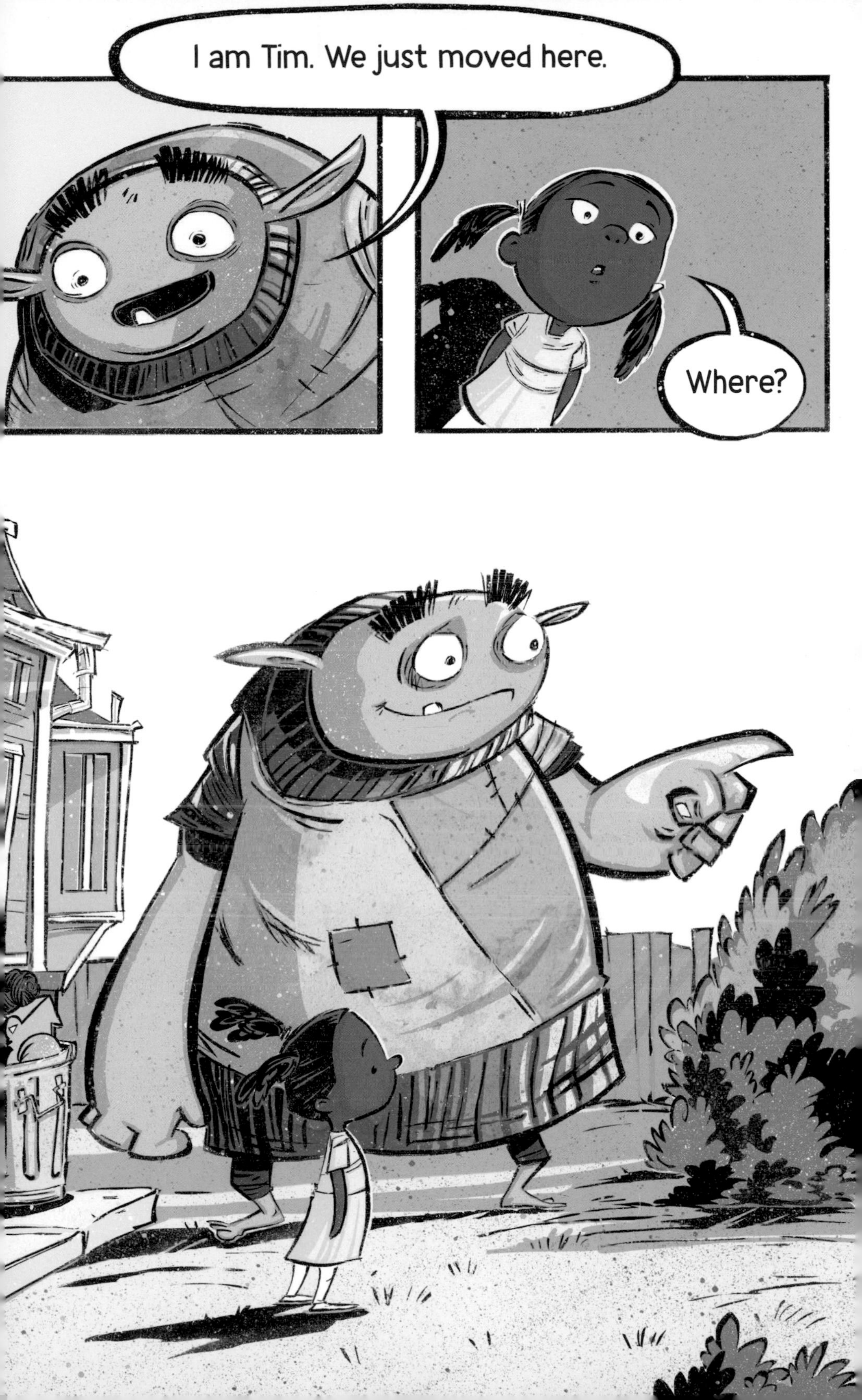
I am Tim. We just moved here.
Where?

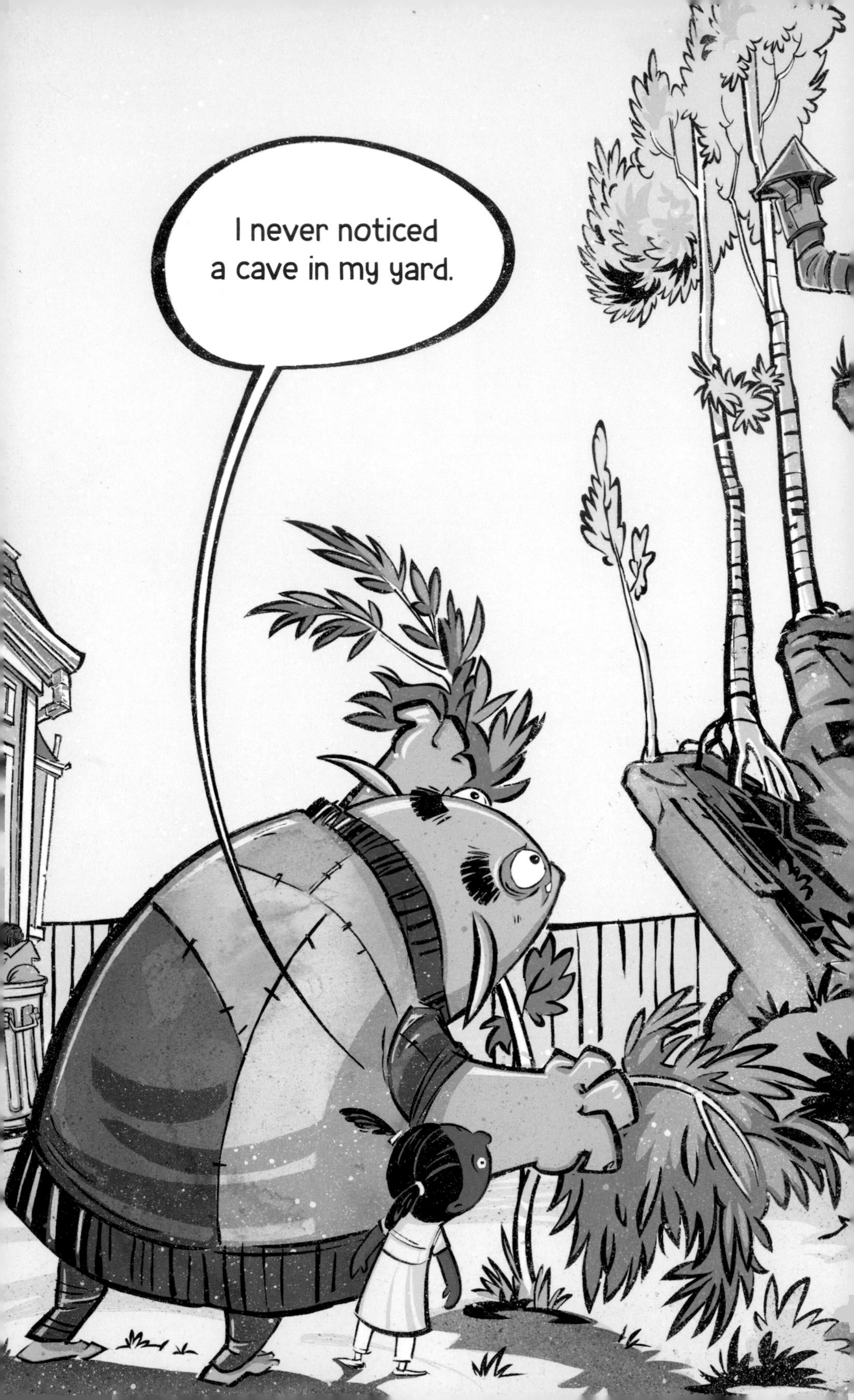
I never noticed a cave in my yard.

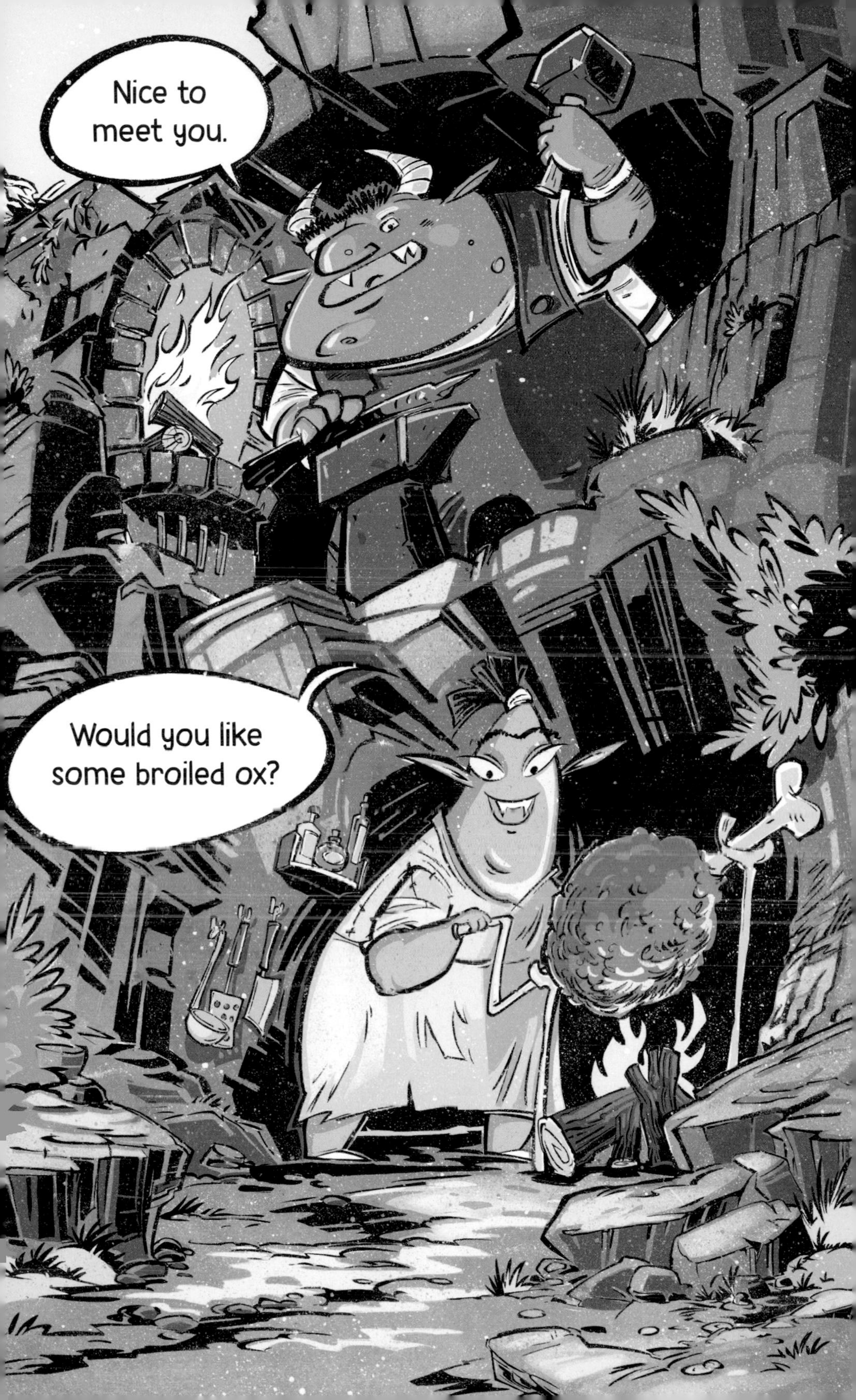
Nice to meet you.
Would you like some broiled ox?

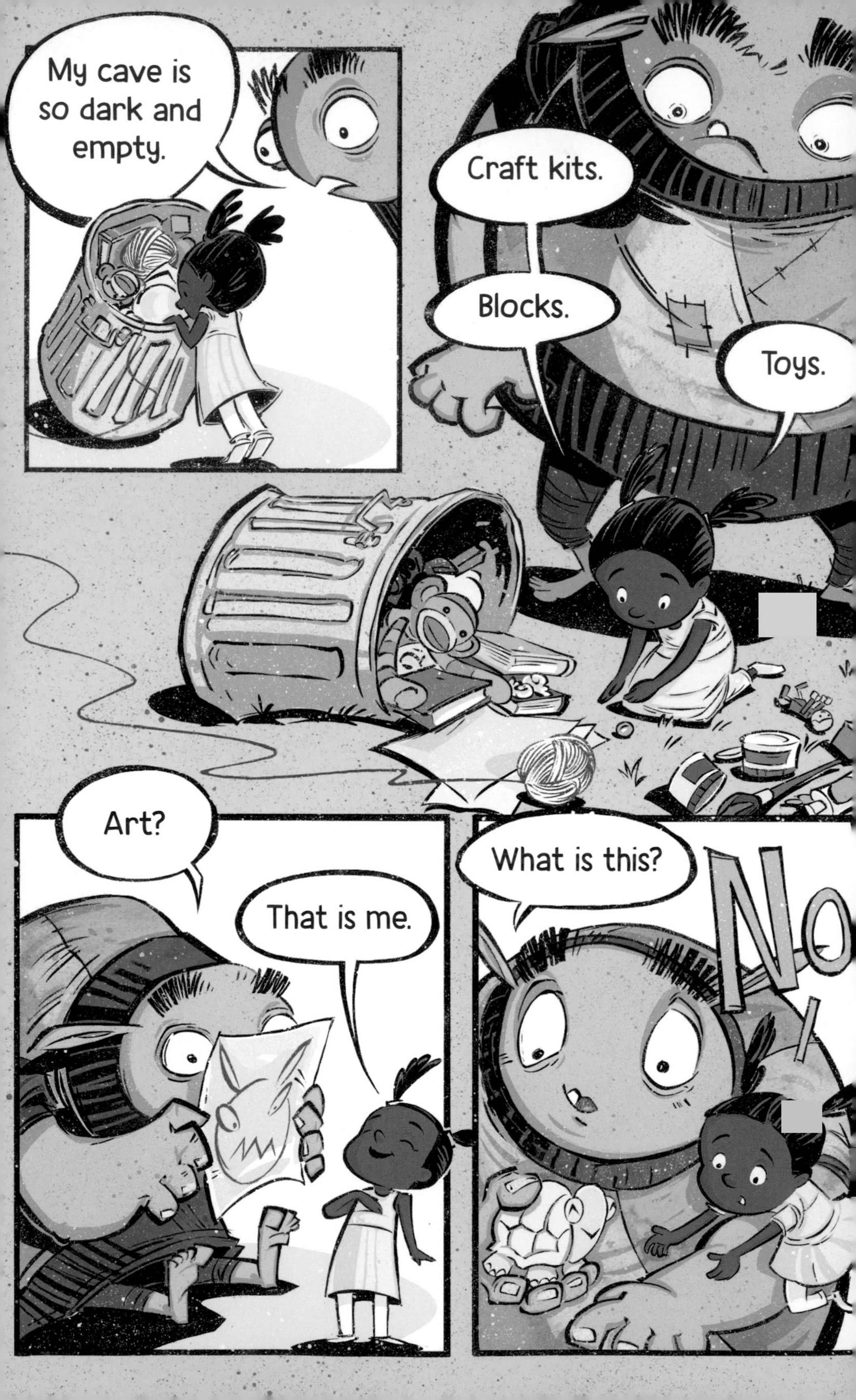
My cave is so dark and empty.
Craft kits.
Blocks.
Toys.
Art?
That is me.
What is this?
NO

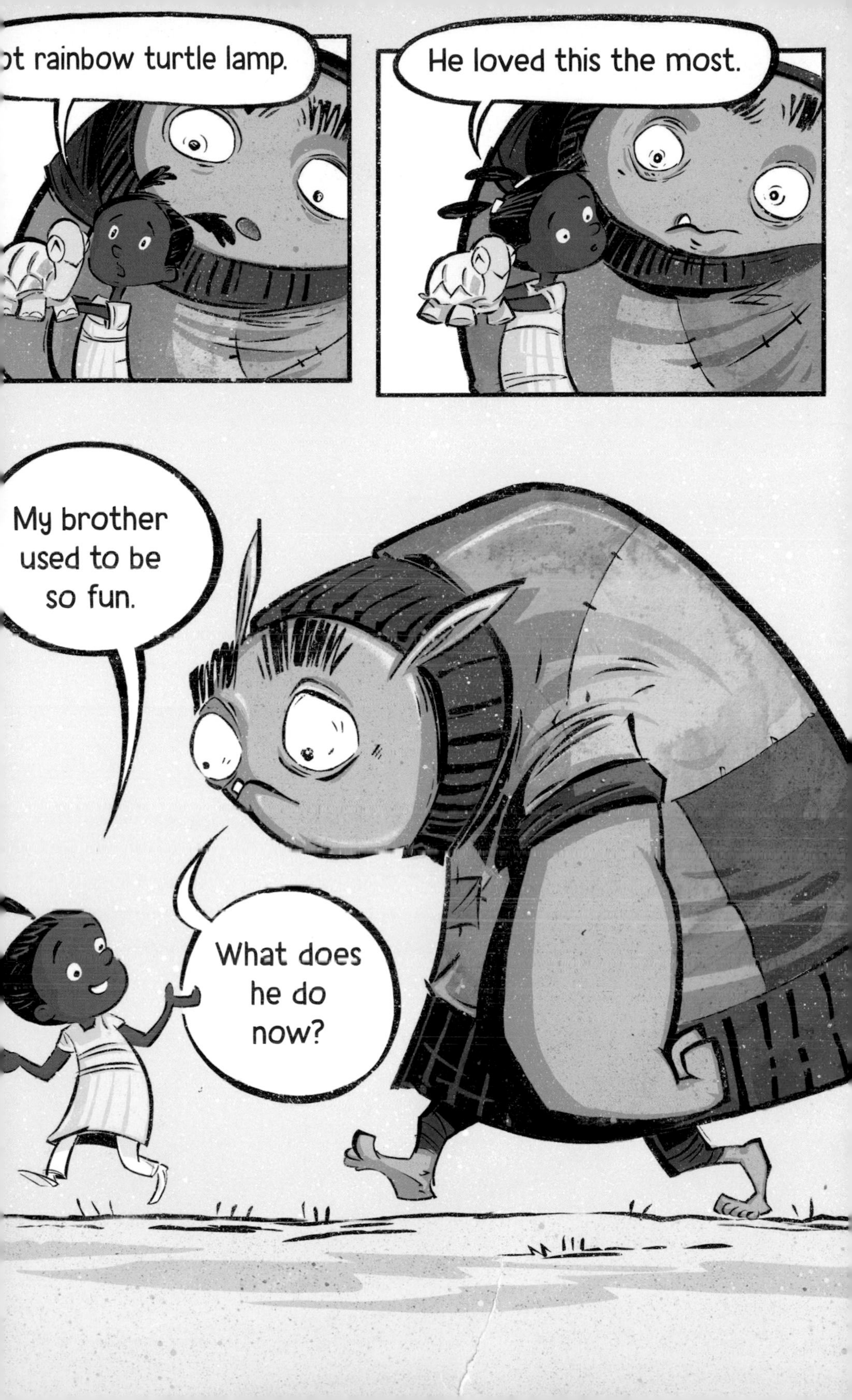
ot rainbow turtle lamp.
He loved this the most.
My brother used to be so fun.
What does he do now?

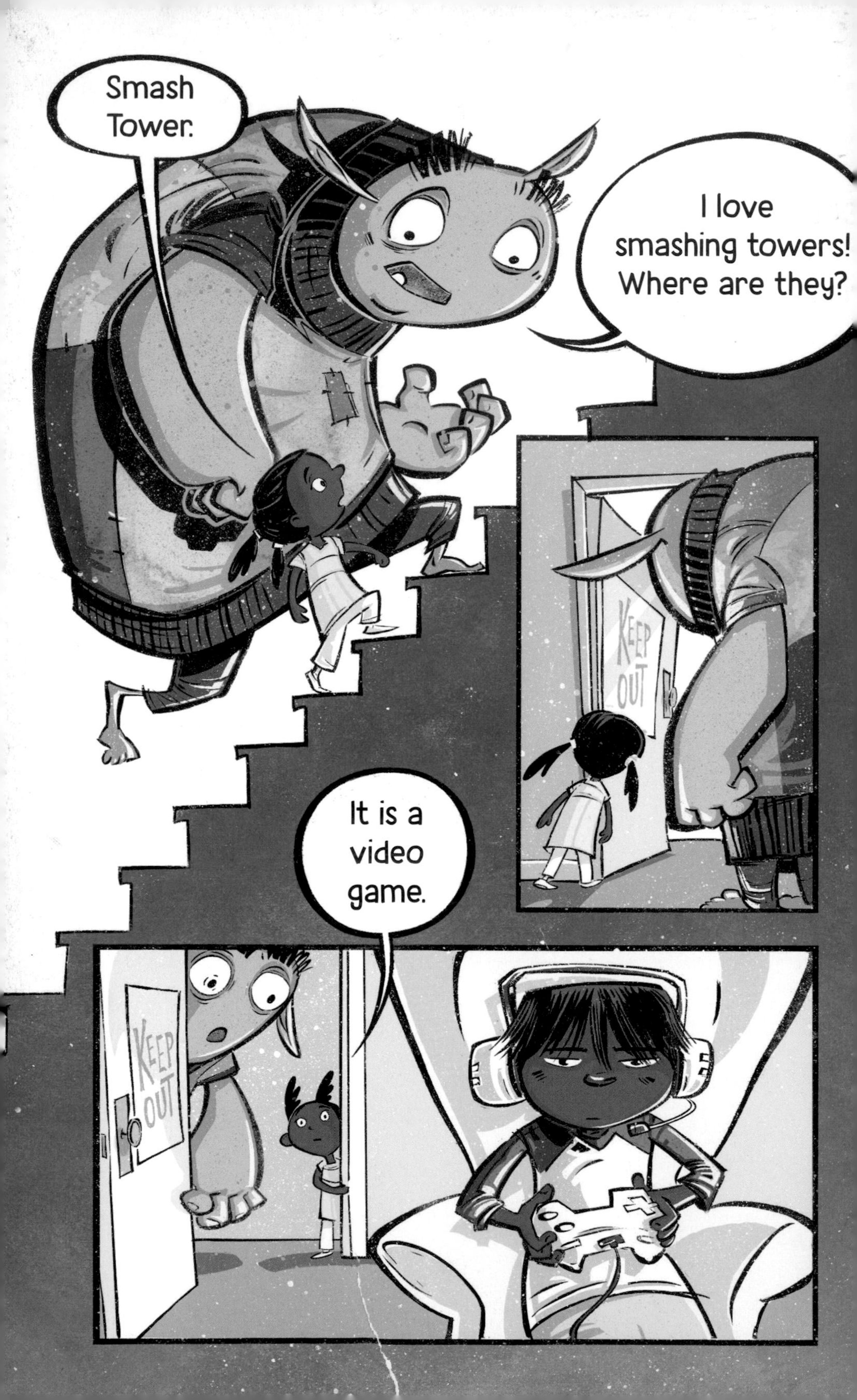
Smash Tower.
I love smashing towers! Where are they?
KEEP OUT
It is a video game.
KEEP OUT

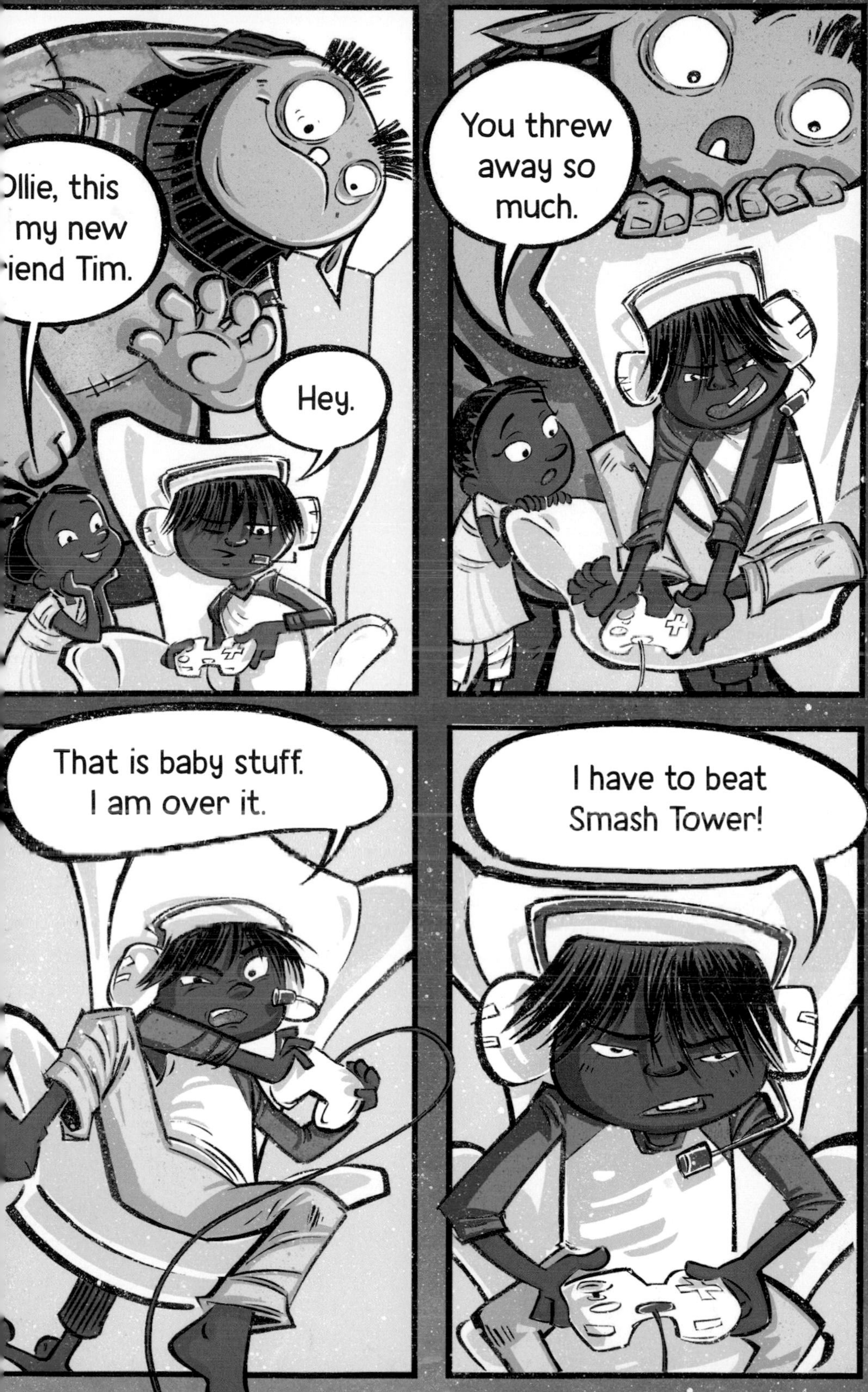
llie, this my new iend Tim.
Hey.
You threw away so much.
That is baby stuff. I am over it.
I have to beat Smash Tower!

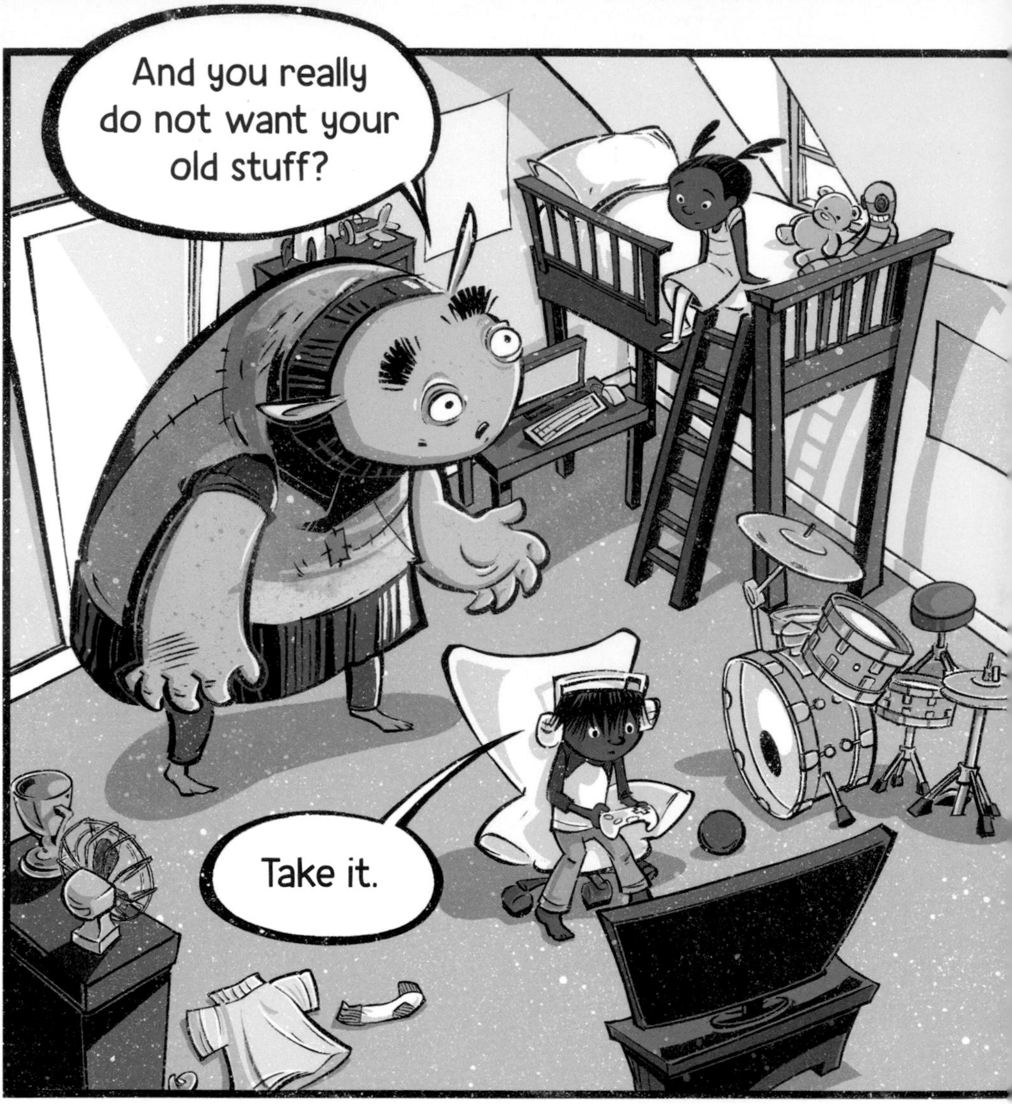
And you really do not want your old stuff?
Take it.

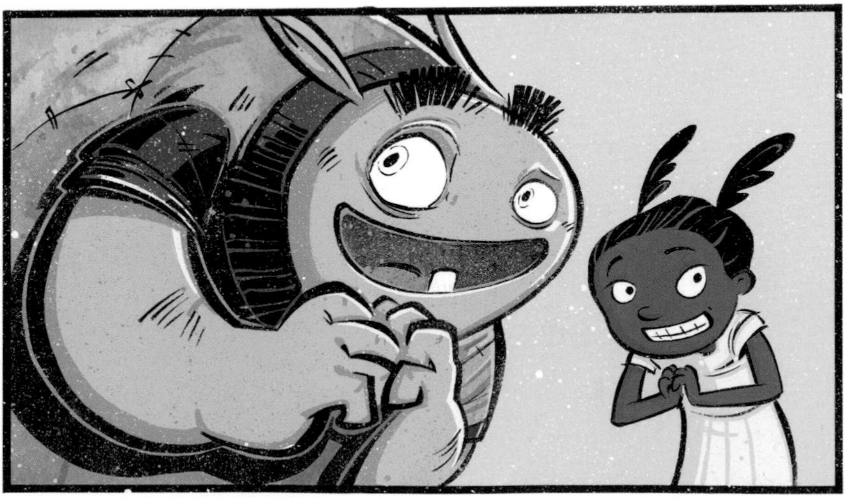

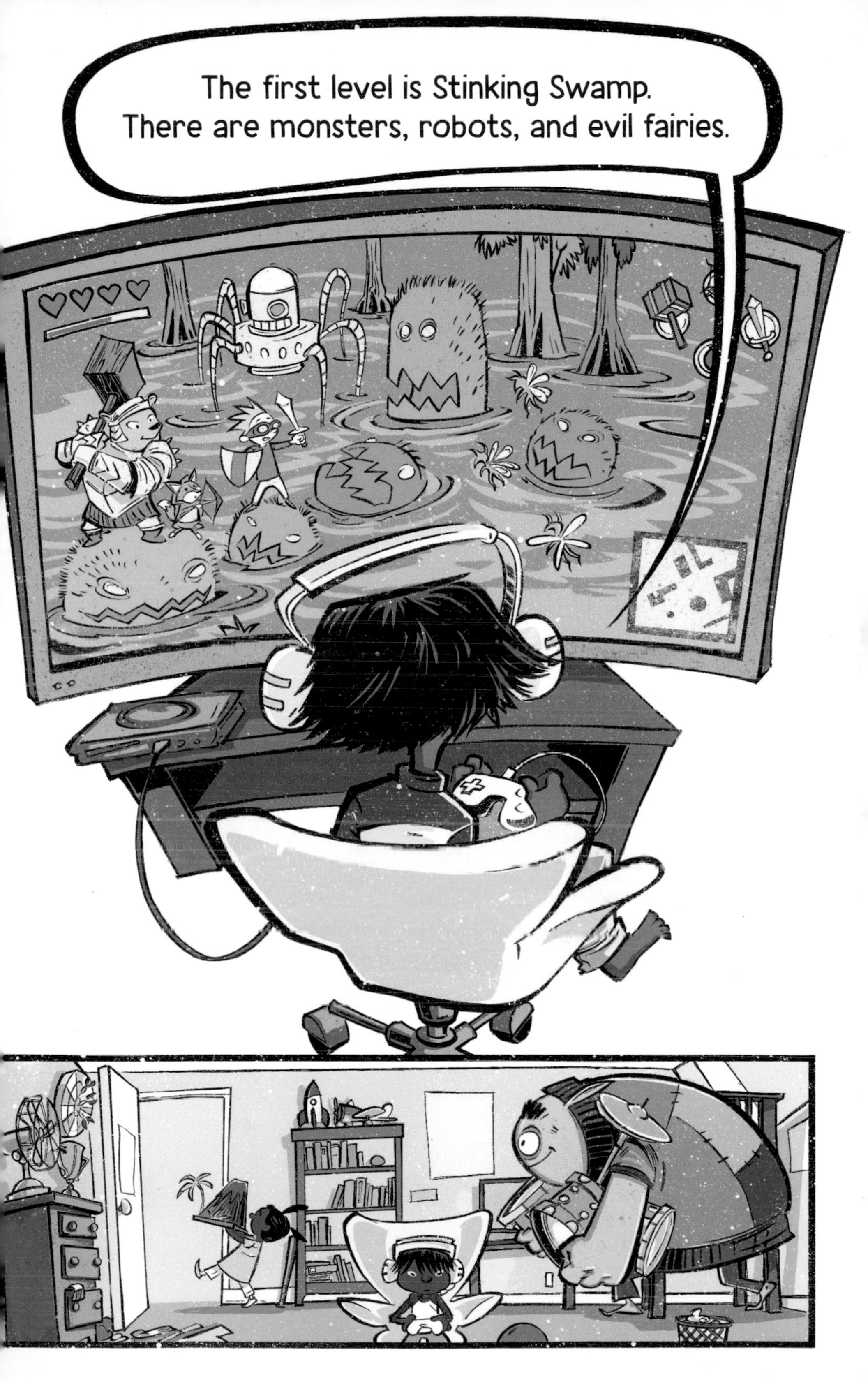
The first level is Stinking Swamp. There are monsters, robots, and evil fairies.

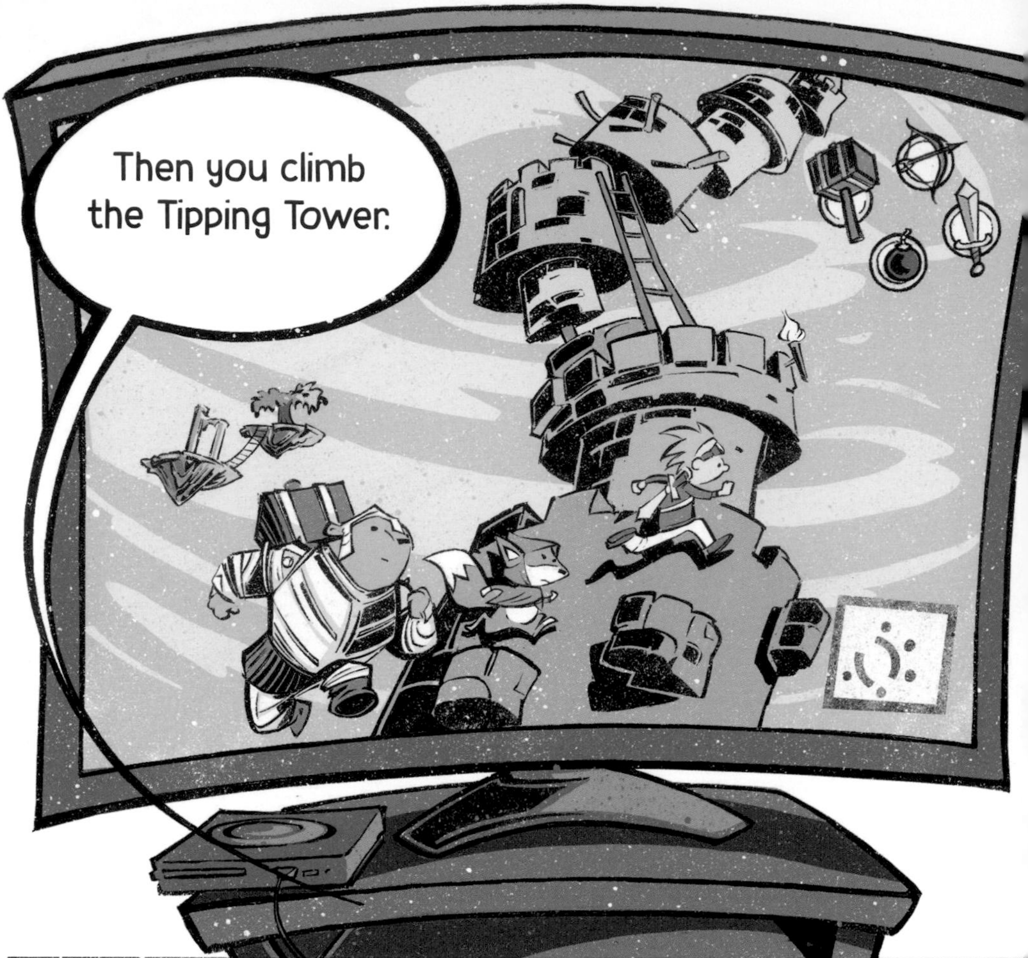
Then you climb the Tipping Tower.

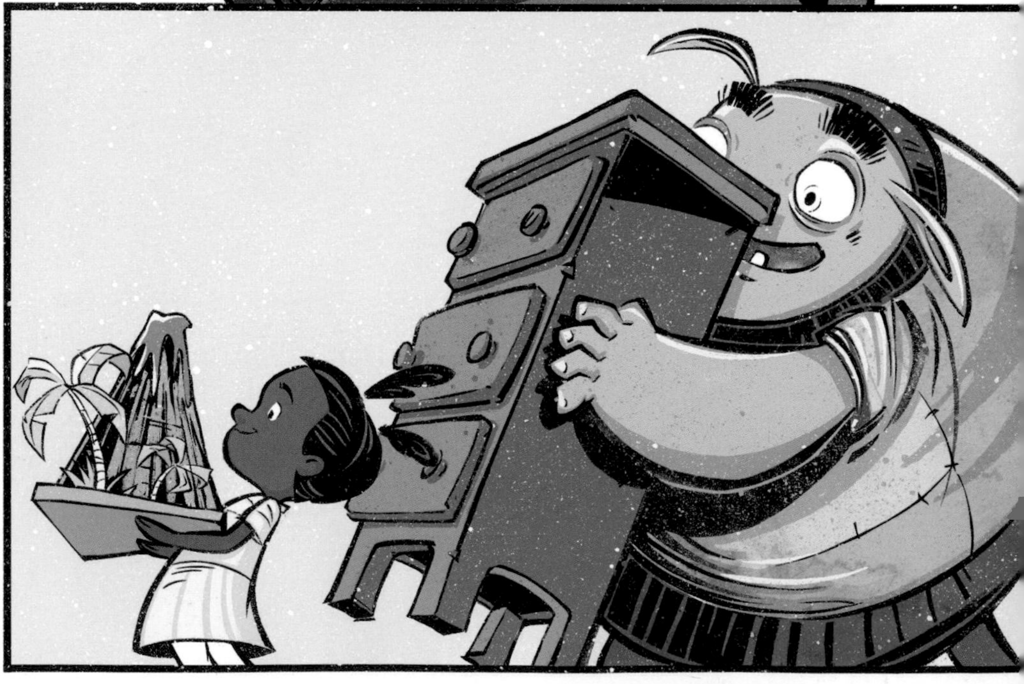

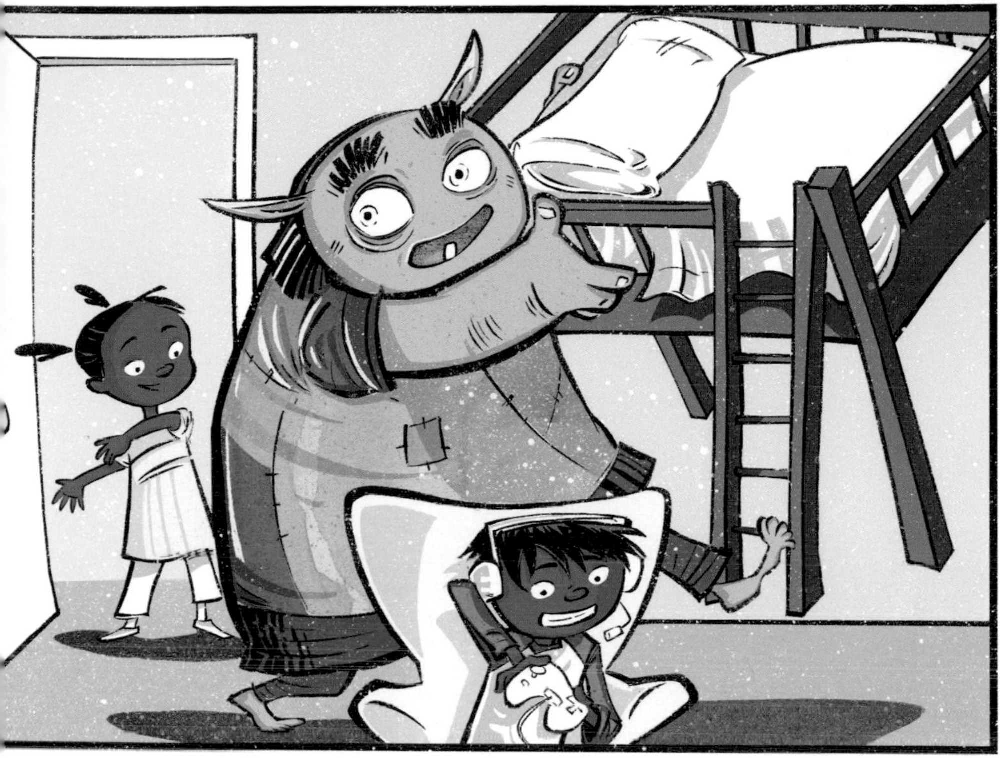

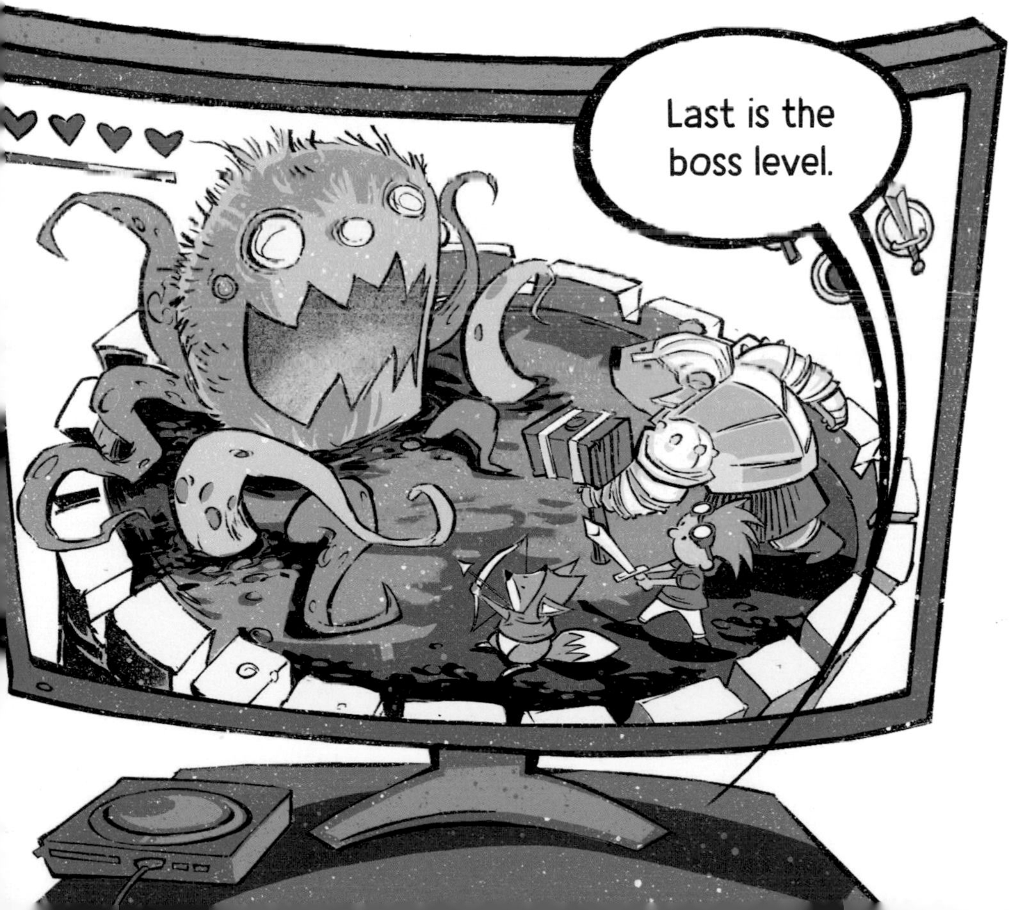
Last is the boss level.

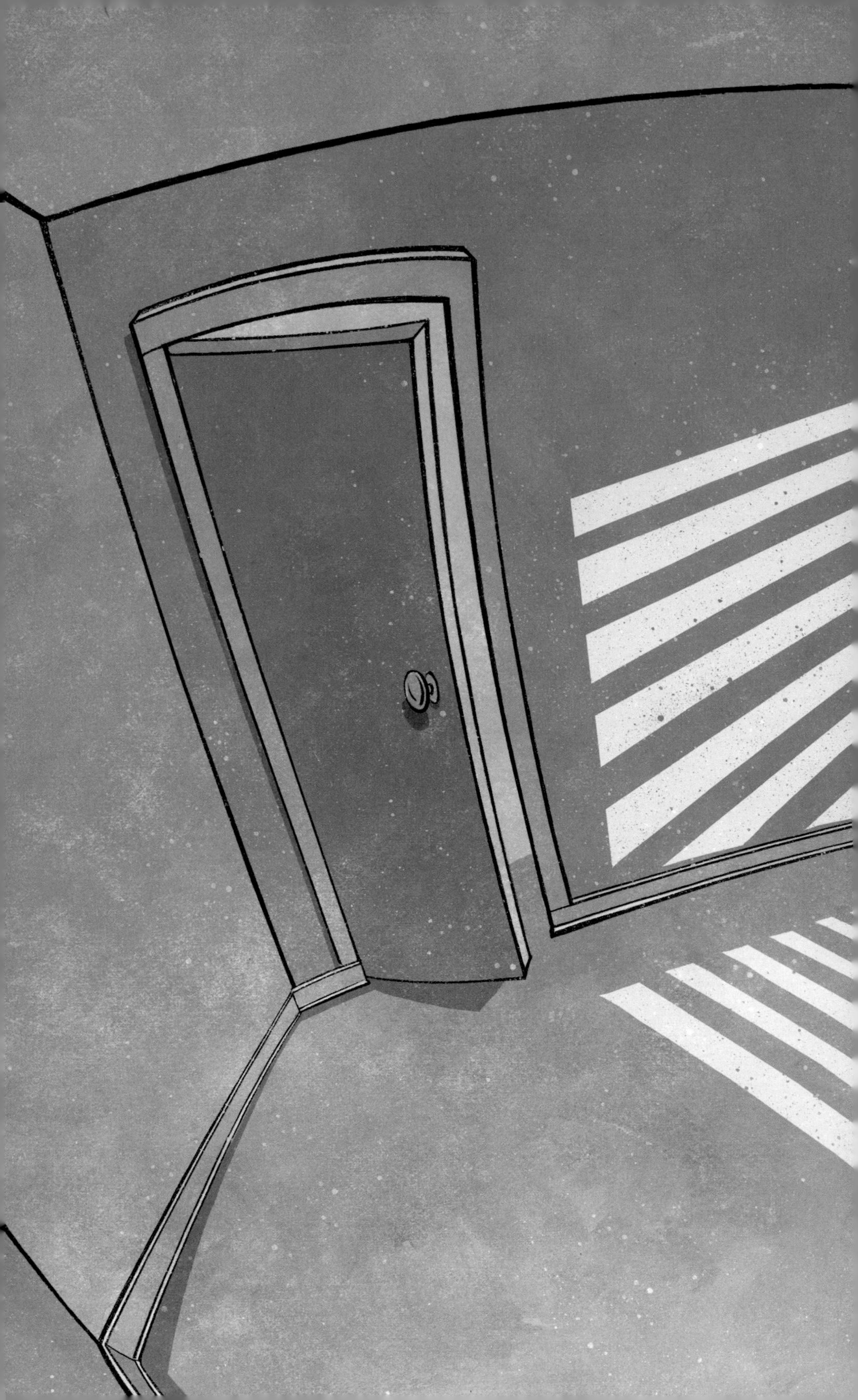

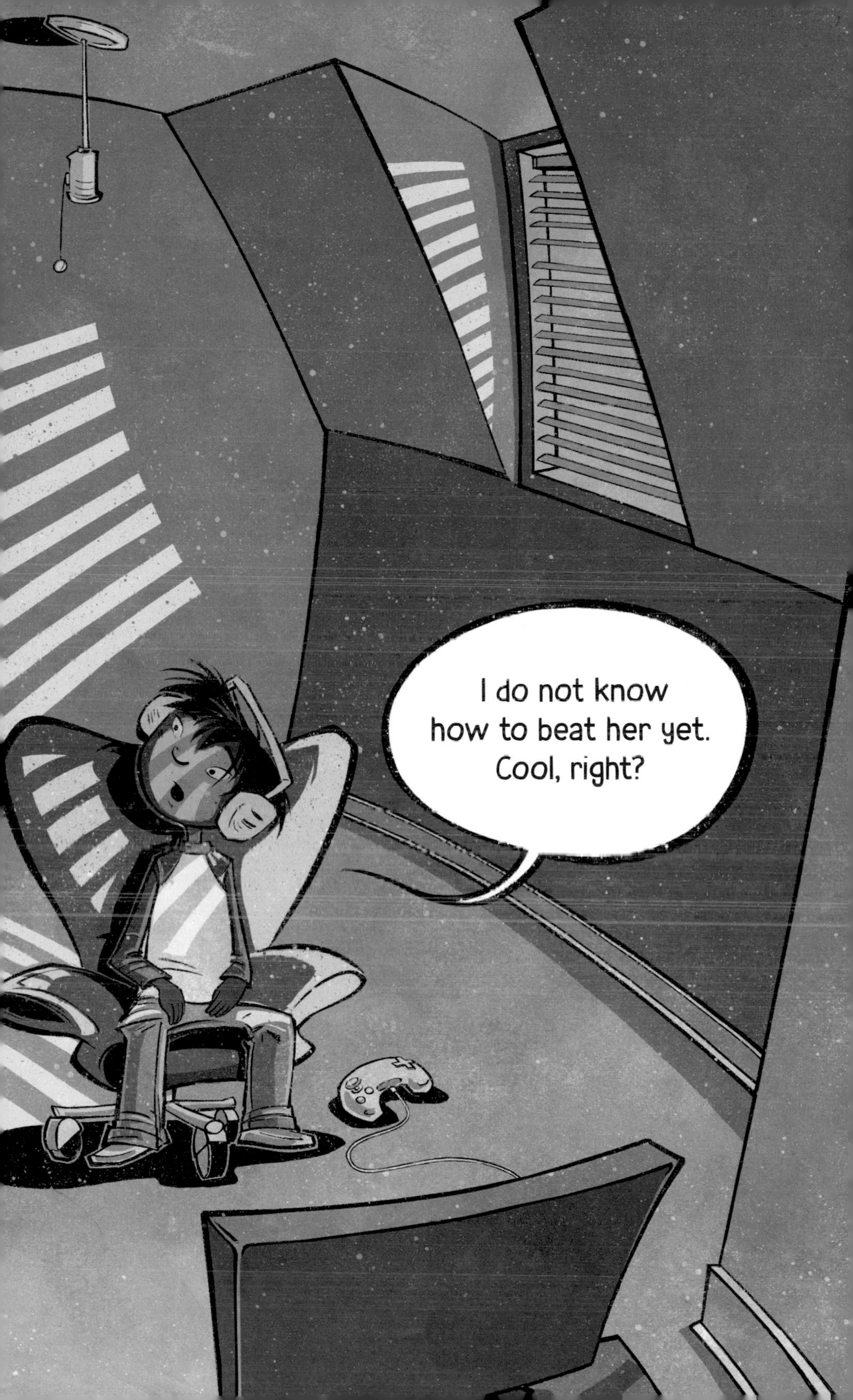
I do not know how to beat her yet. Cool, right?

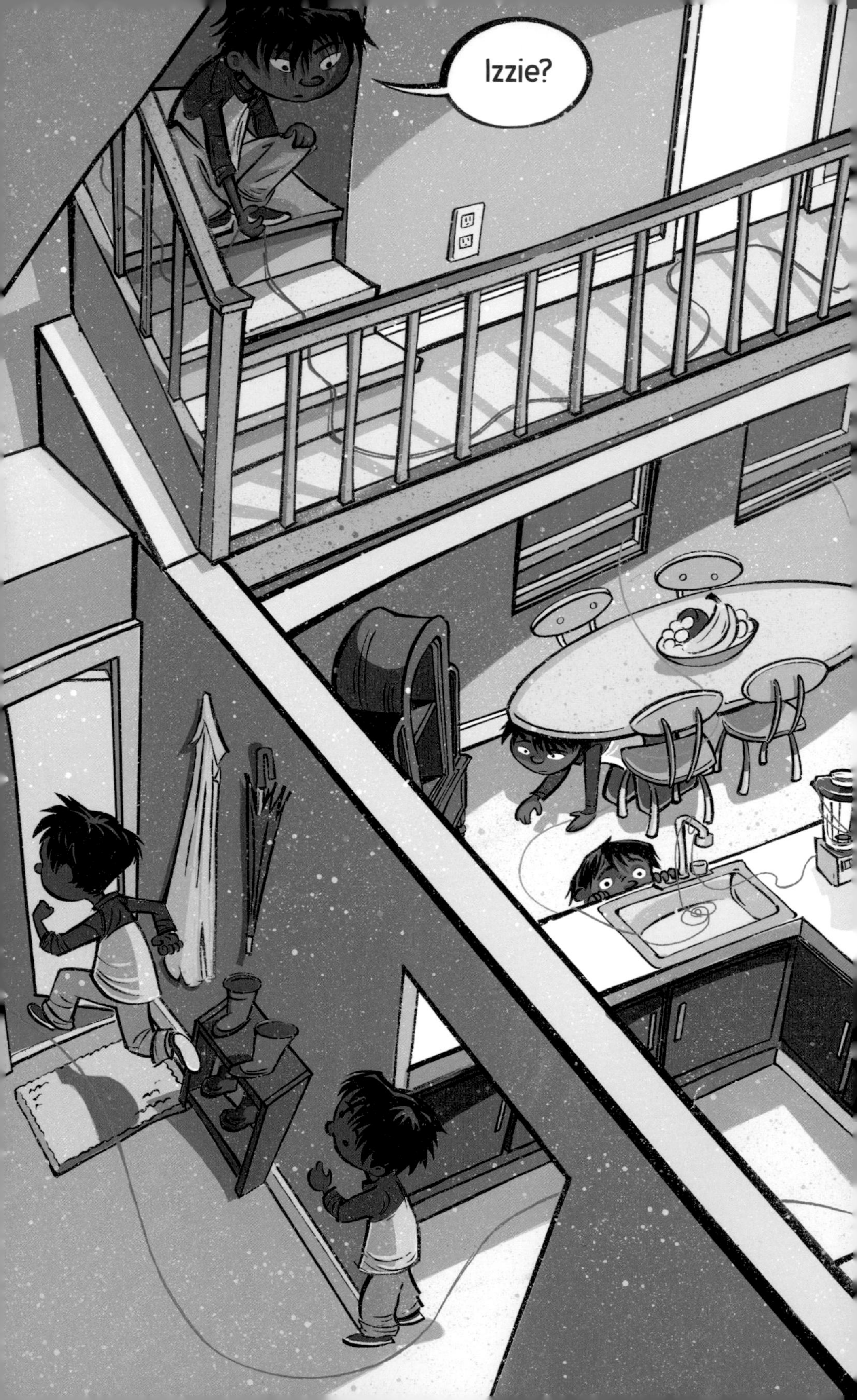
Izzie?

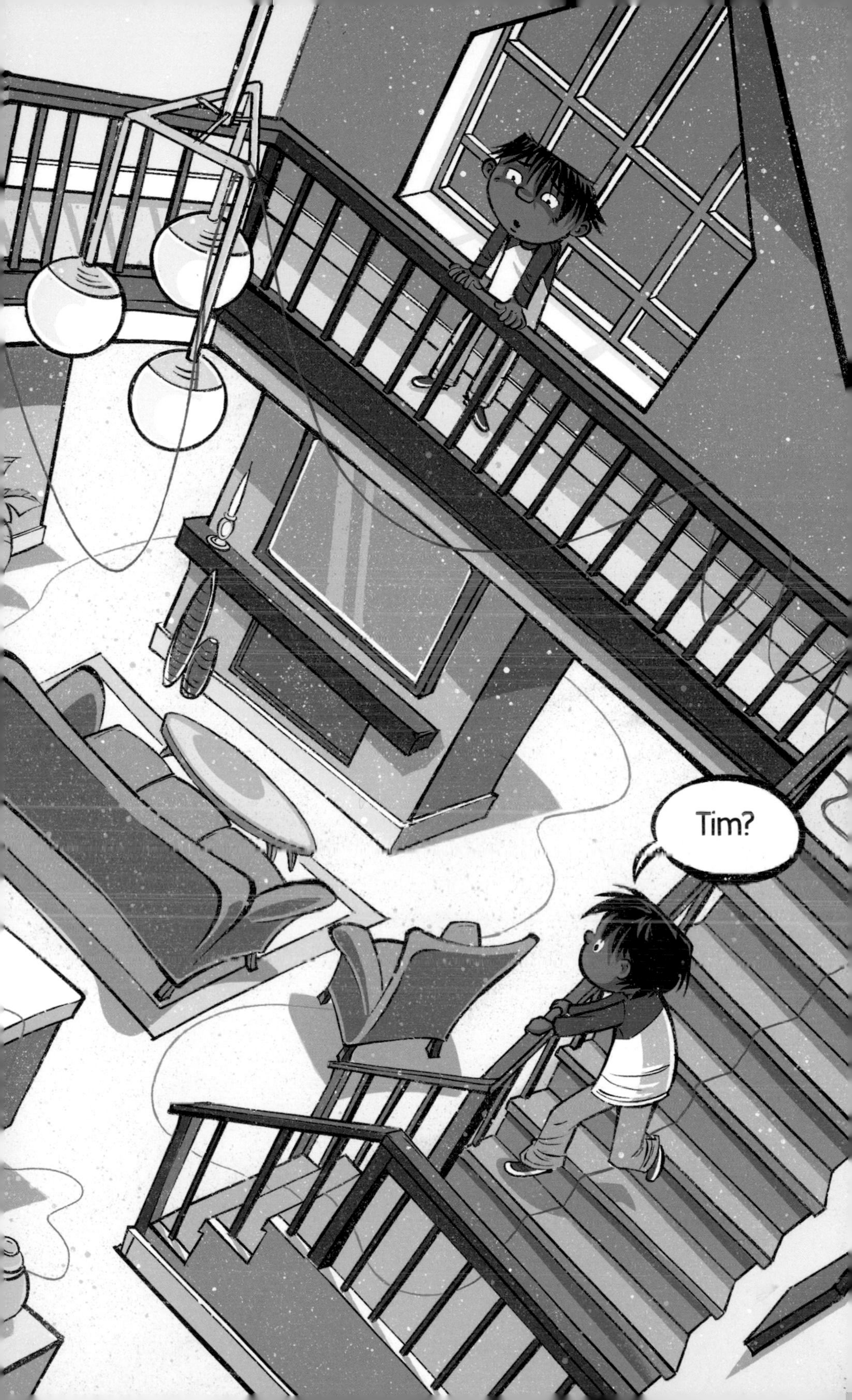
Tim?

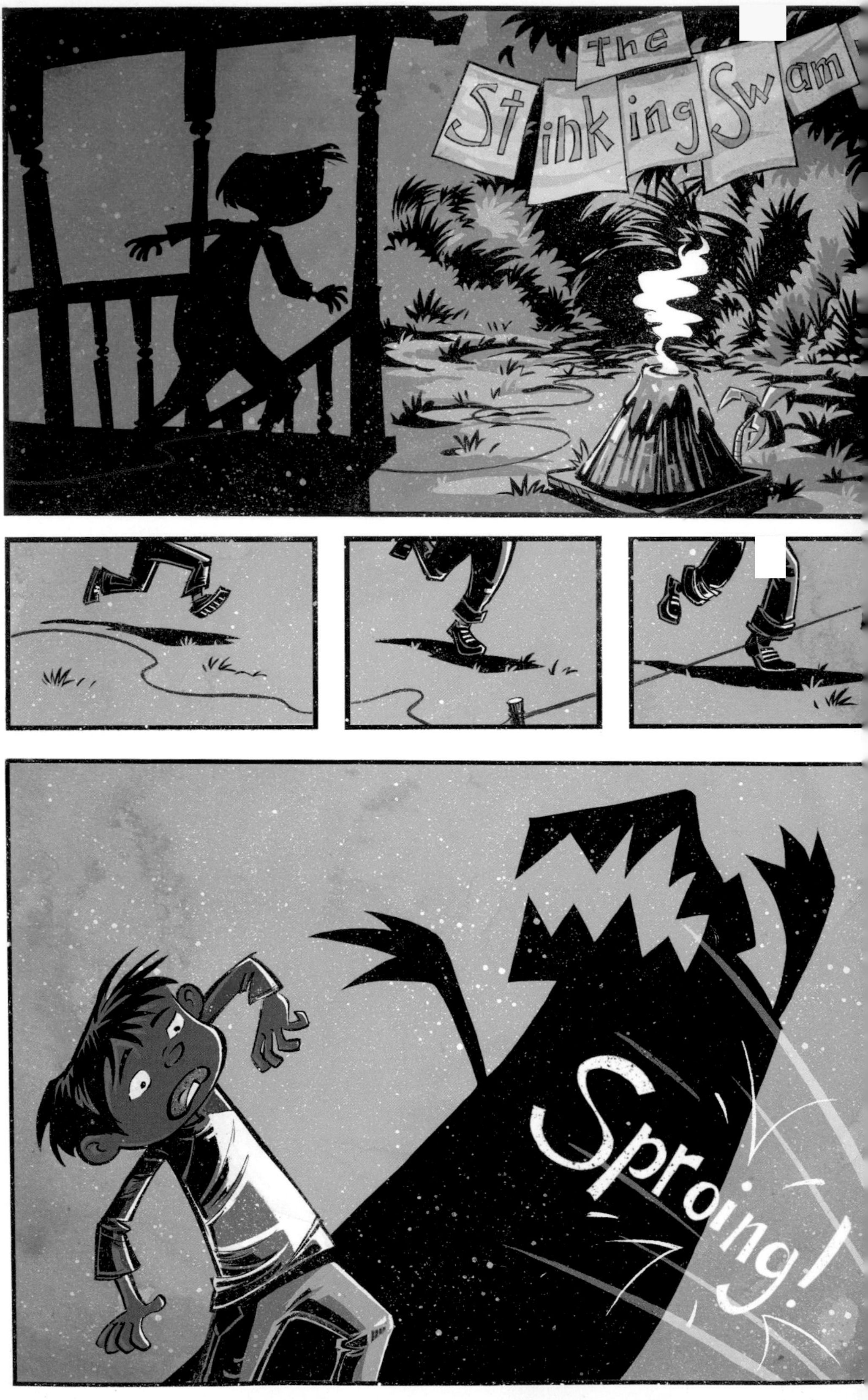
The
Stinking Swam
Sproing!

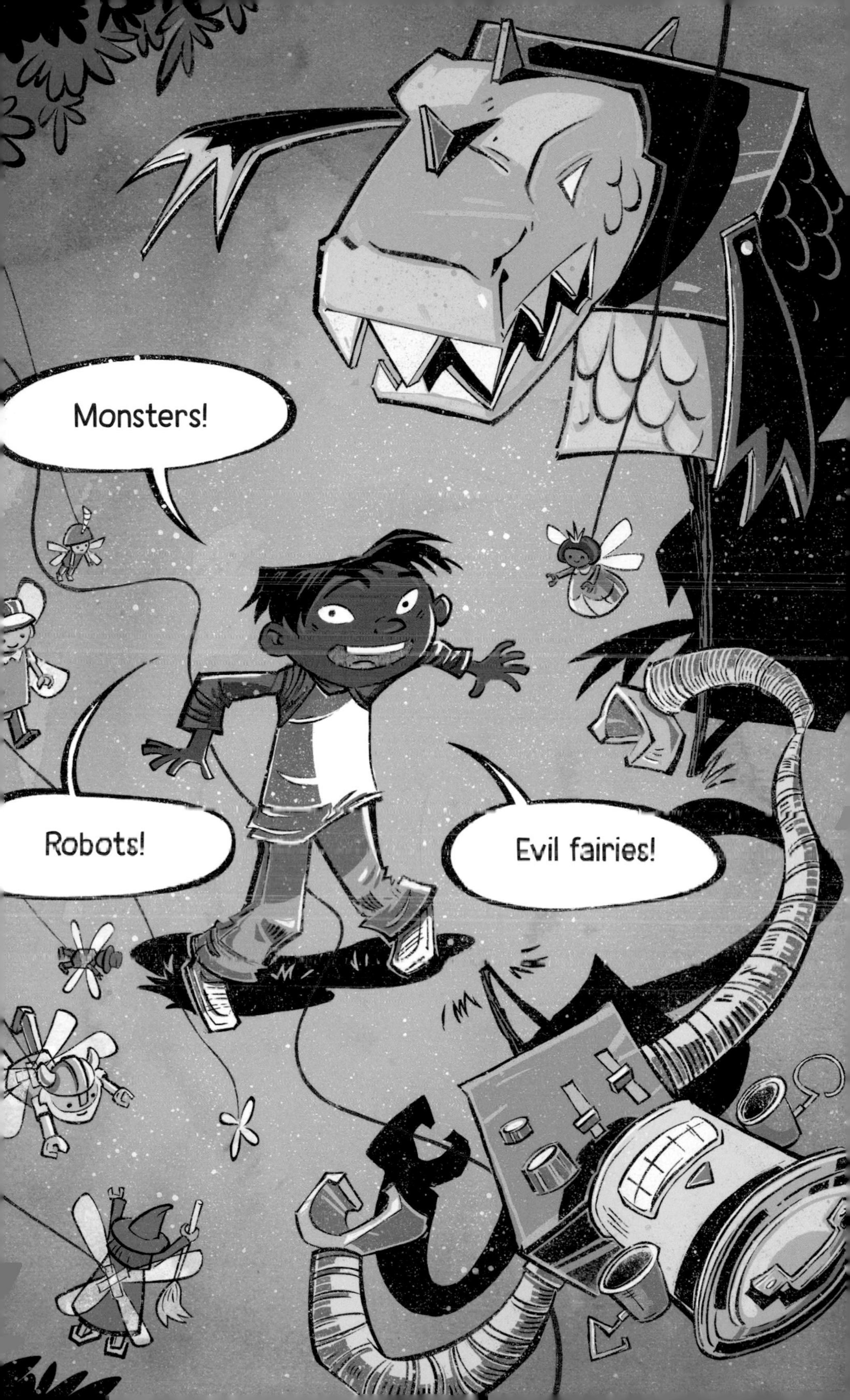
Monsters!
Robots!
Evil fairies!

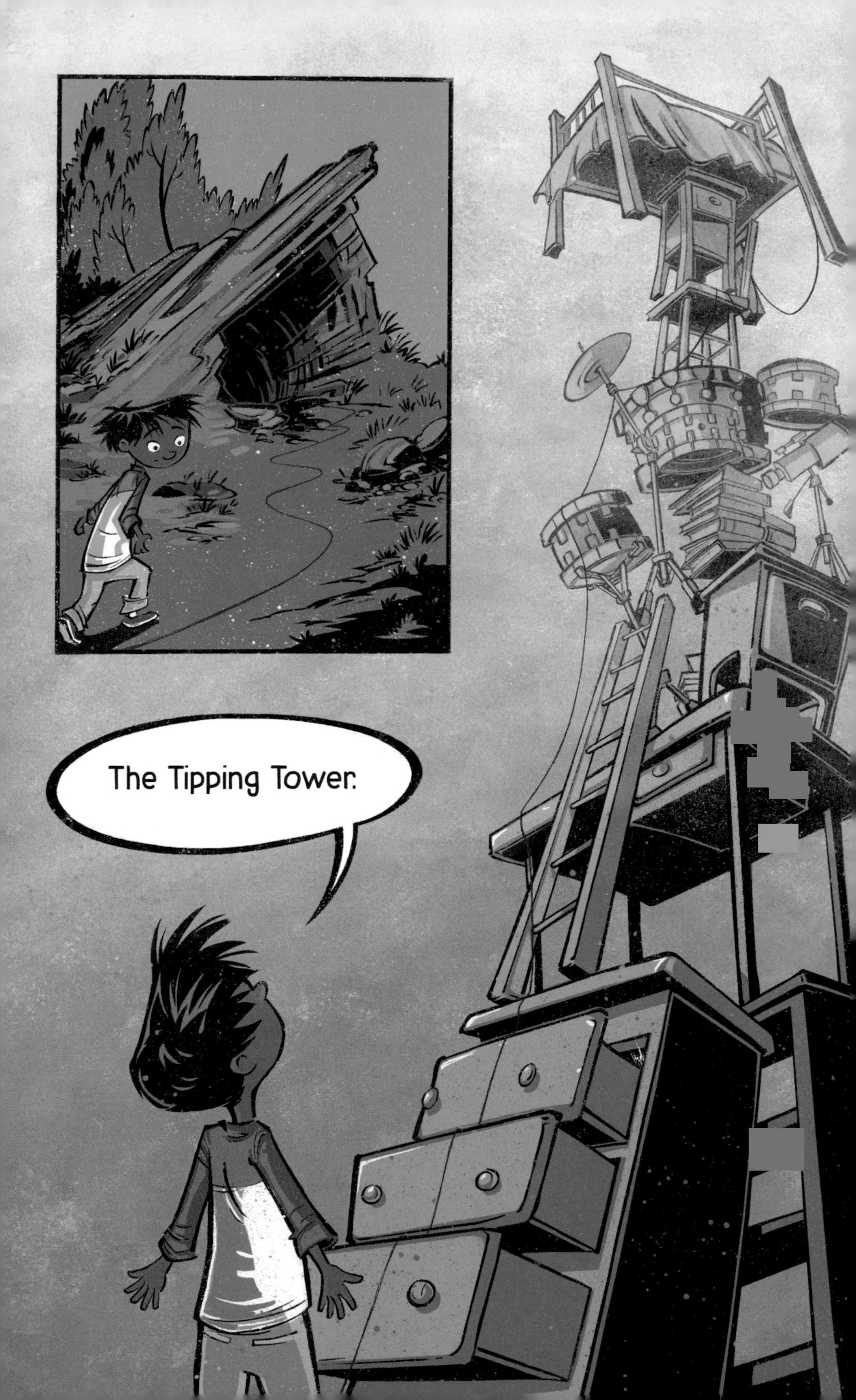
The Tipping Tower.

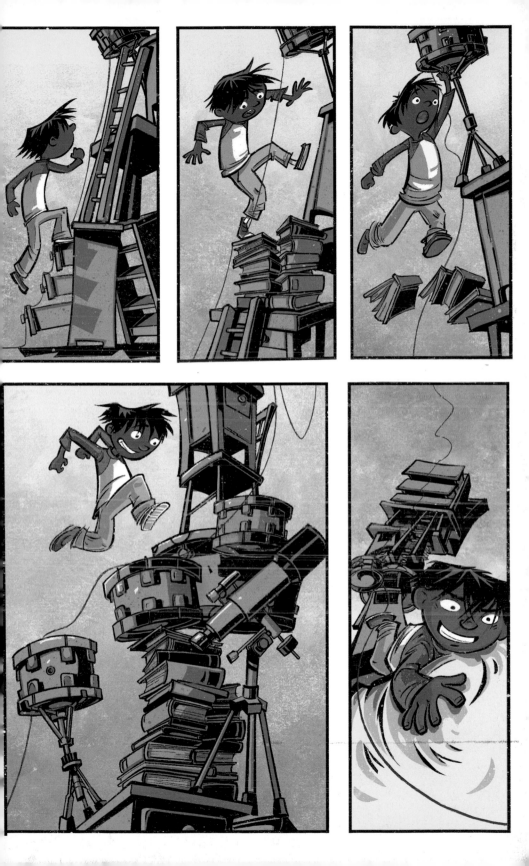

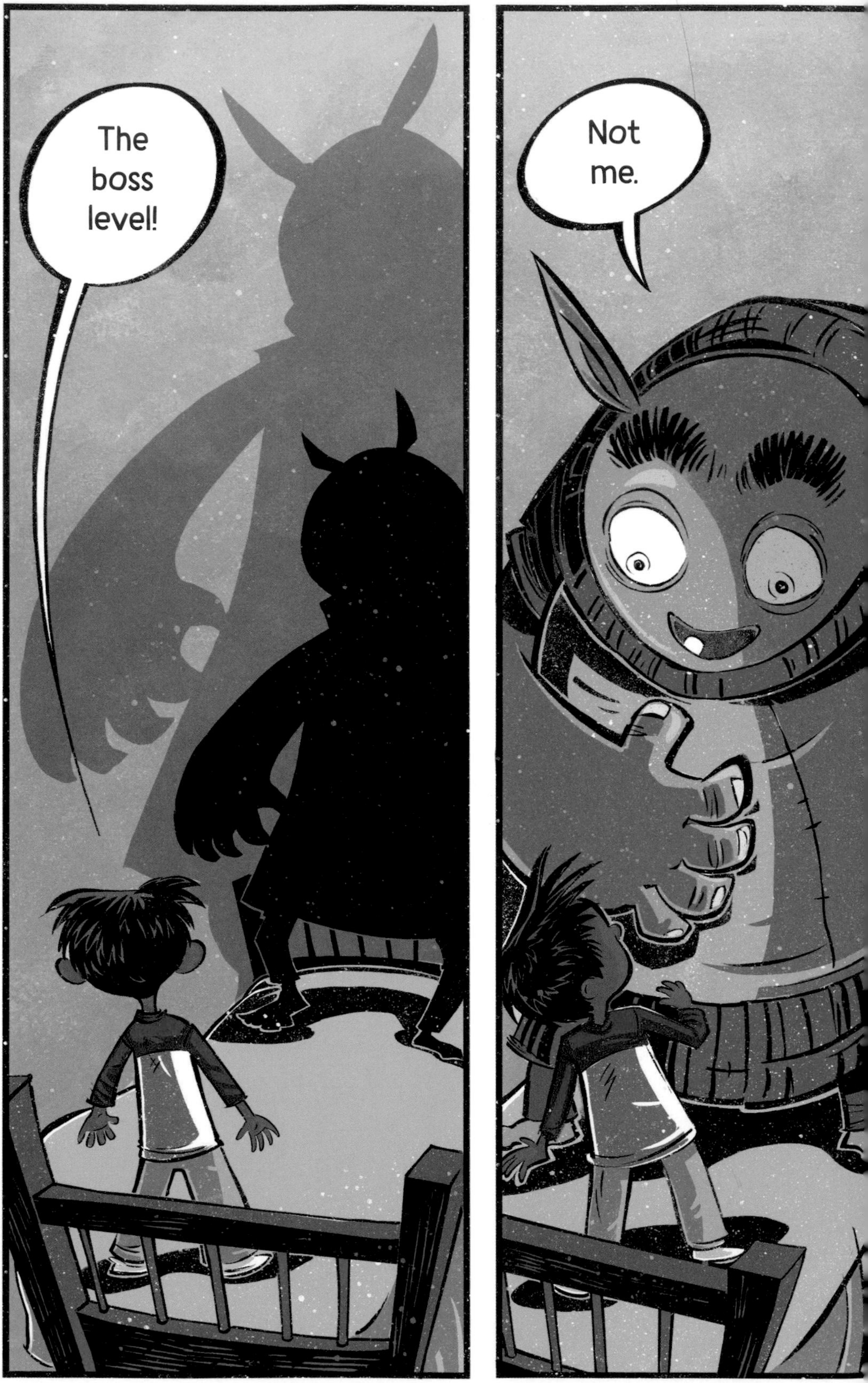
The boss level!
Not me.

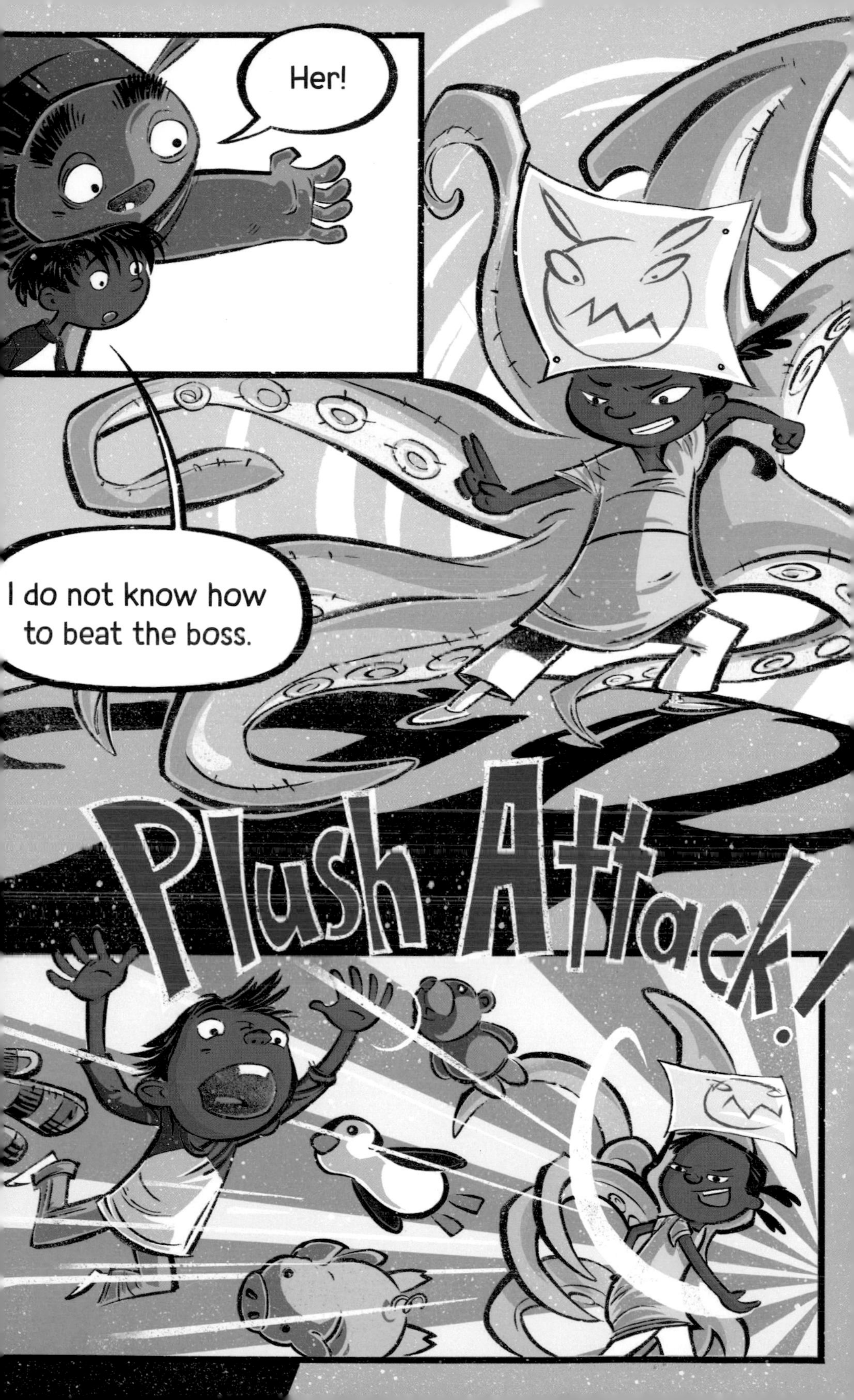
Her!
I do not know how to beat the boss.
Plush Attack!

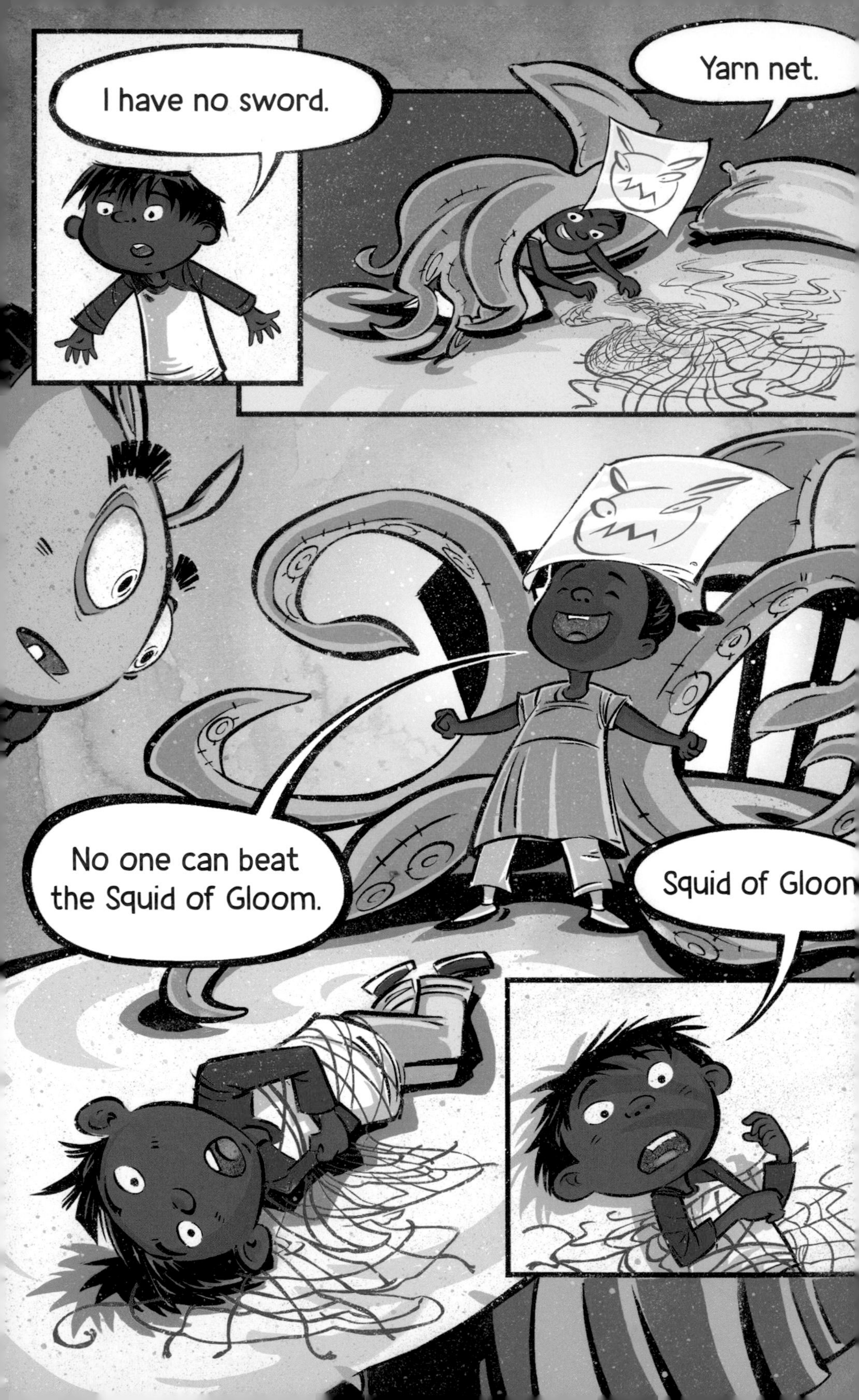
I have no sword.
Yarn net.
No one can beat the Squid of Gloom.
Squid of Gloon

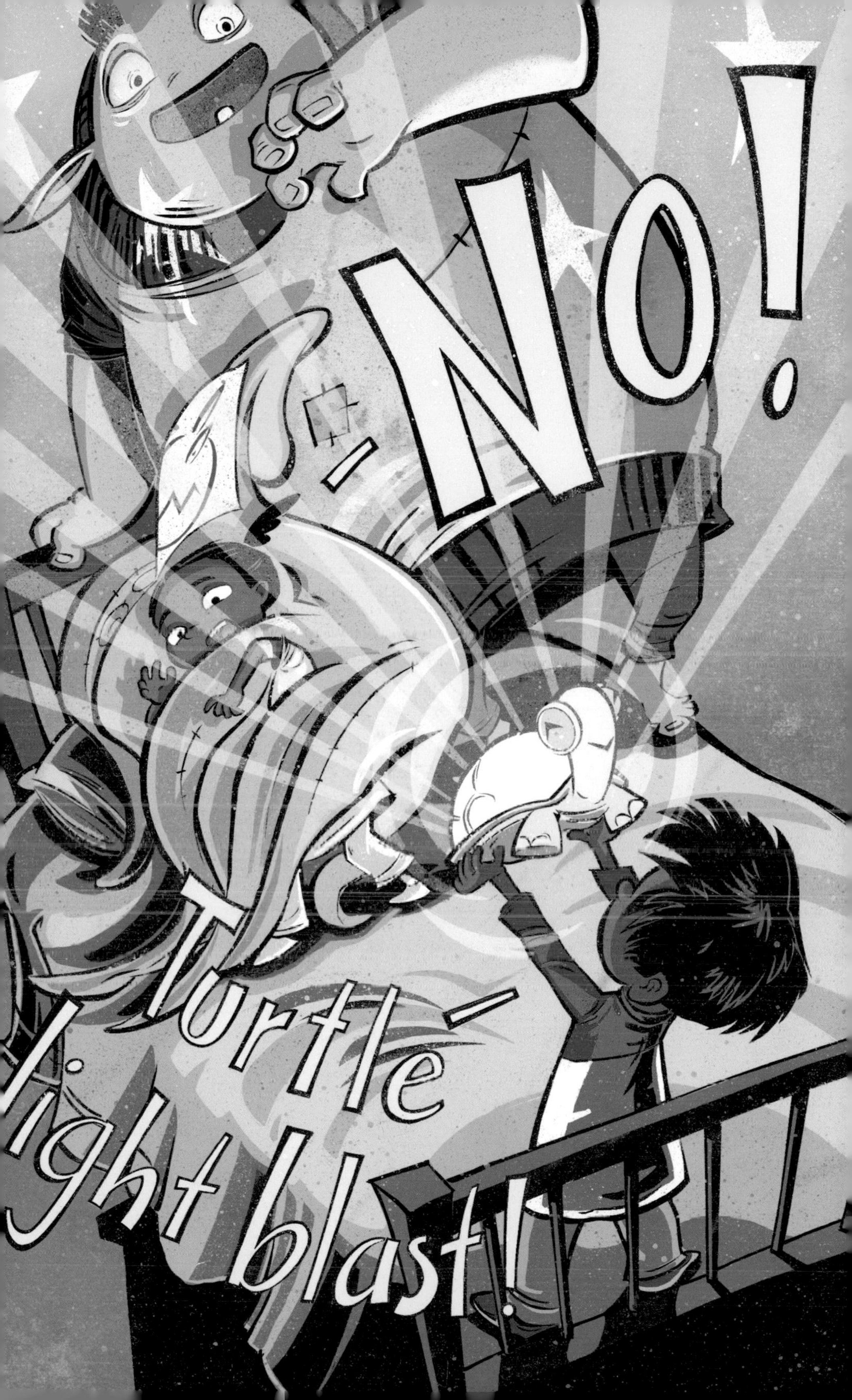
NO!
Turtle-light blast!

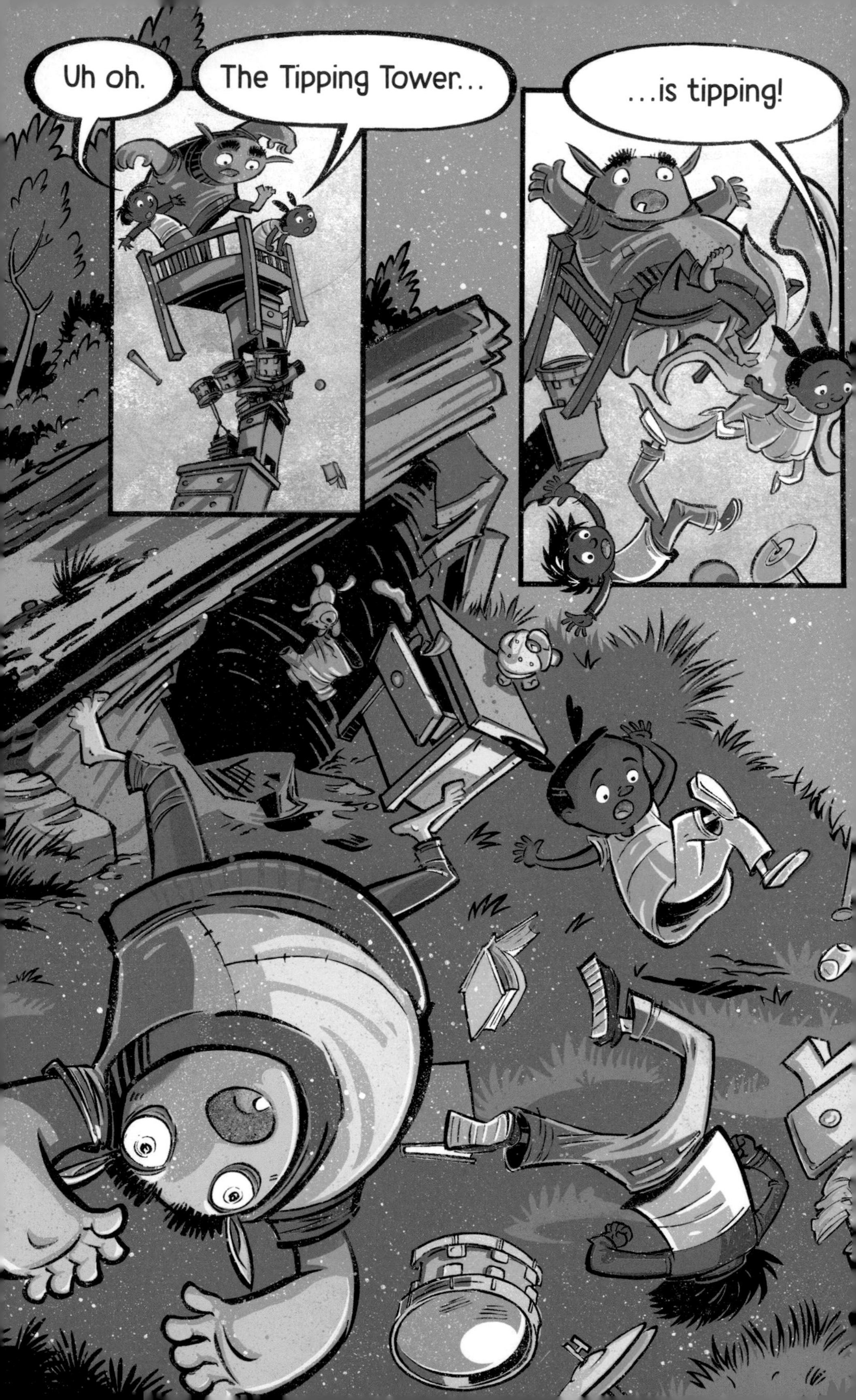
Uh oh.
The Tipping Tower...
...is tipping!

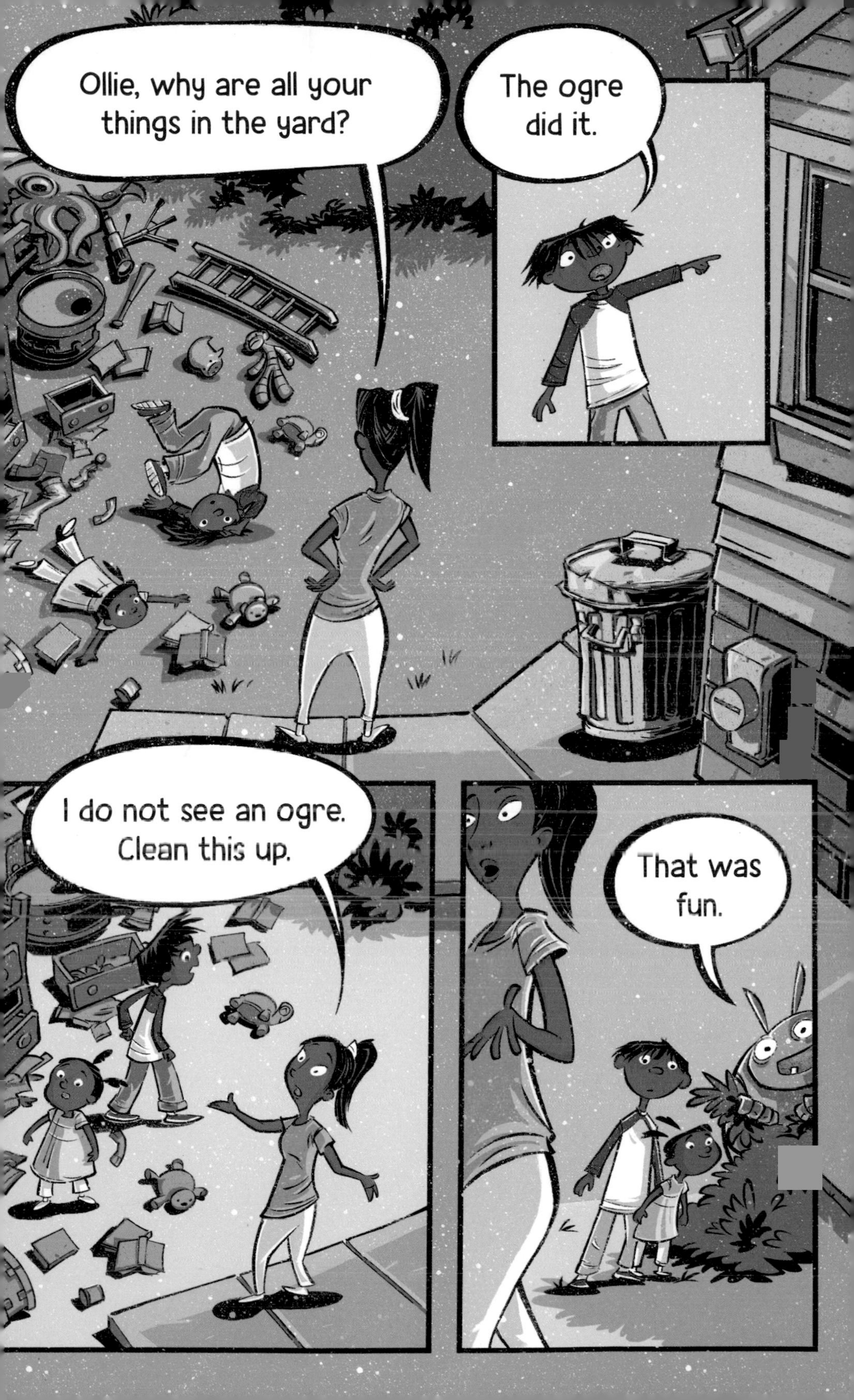
Ollie, why are all your things in the yard?
The ogre did it.
I do not see an ogre. Clean this up.
That was fun.

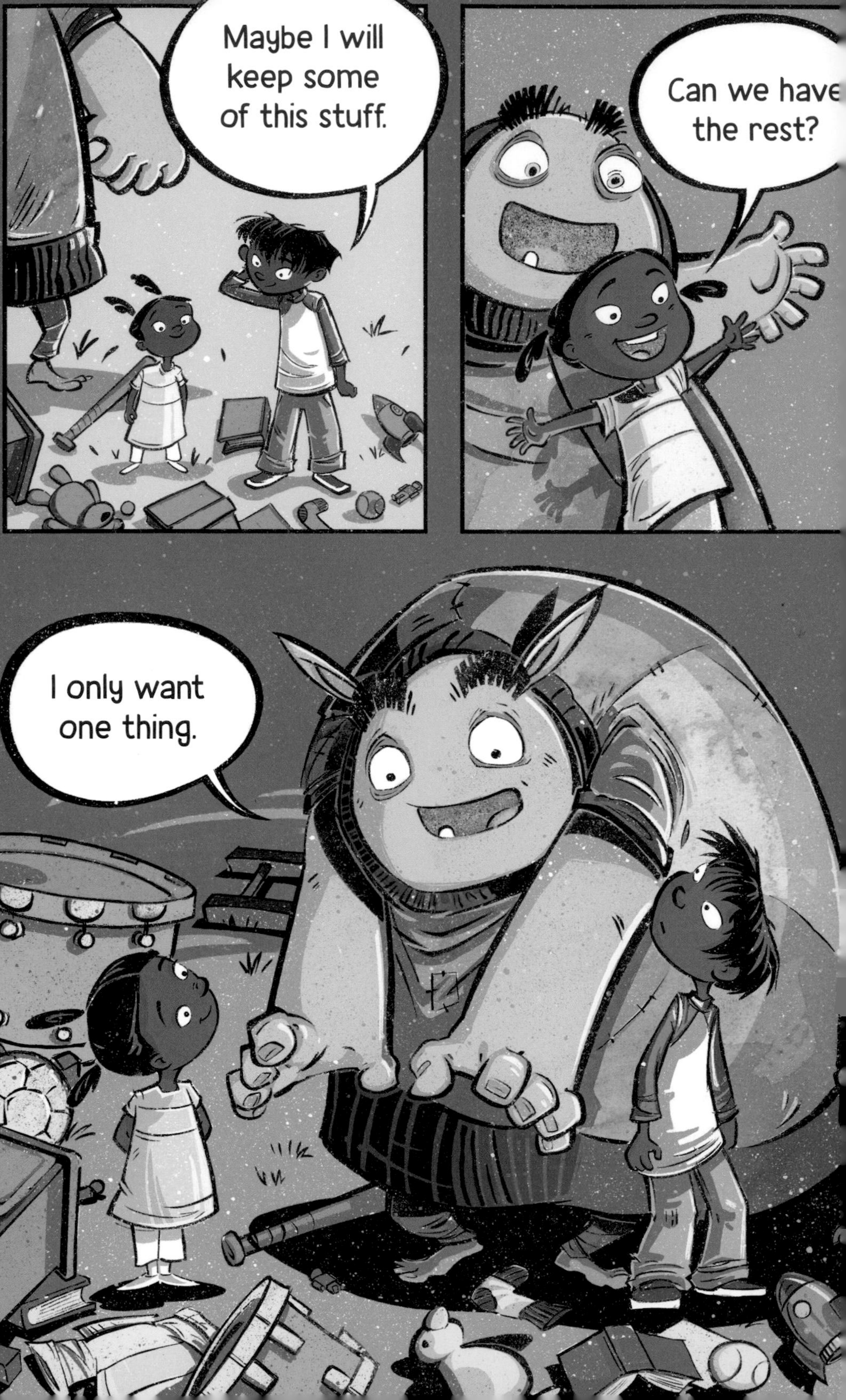
Maybe I will keep some of this stuff.
Can we have the rest?
I only want one thing.

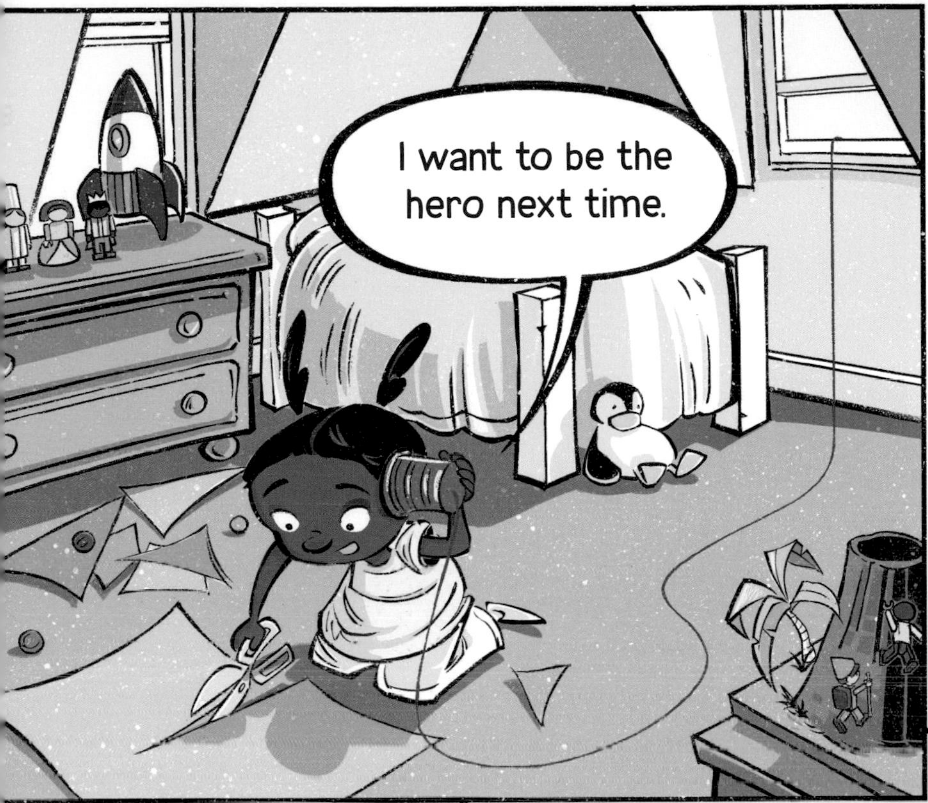
I want to be the hero next time.

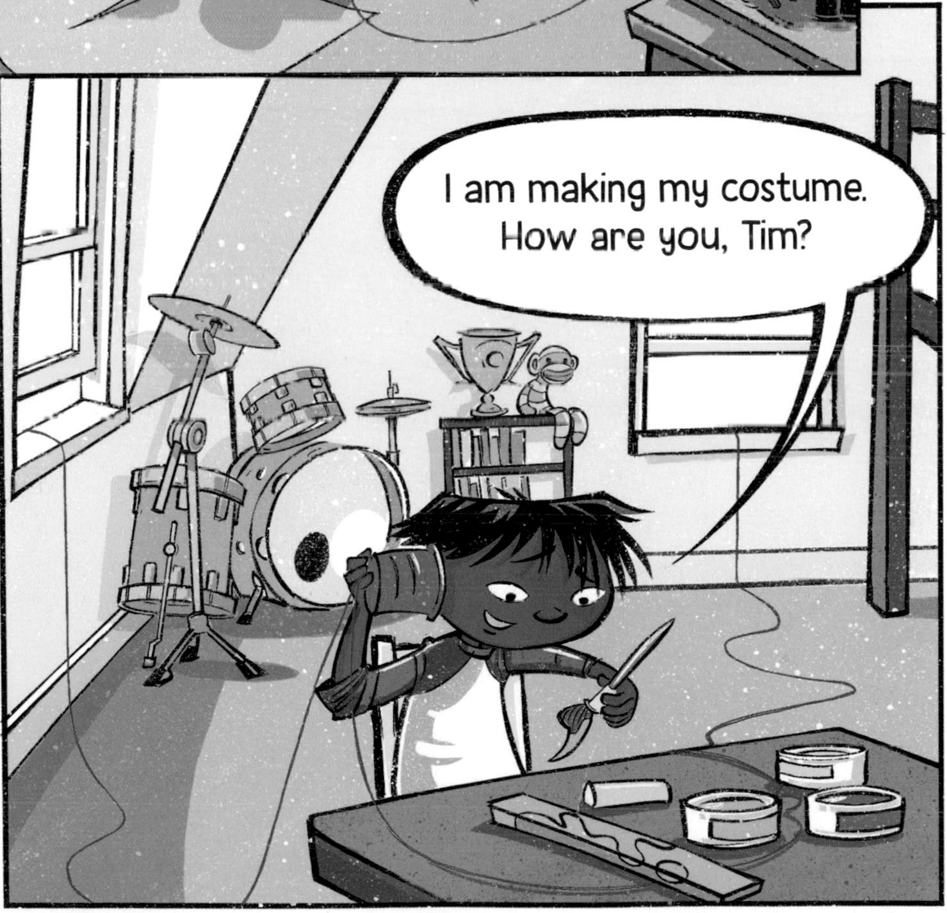
I am making my costume. How are you, Tim?

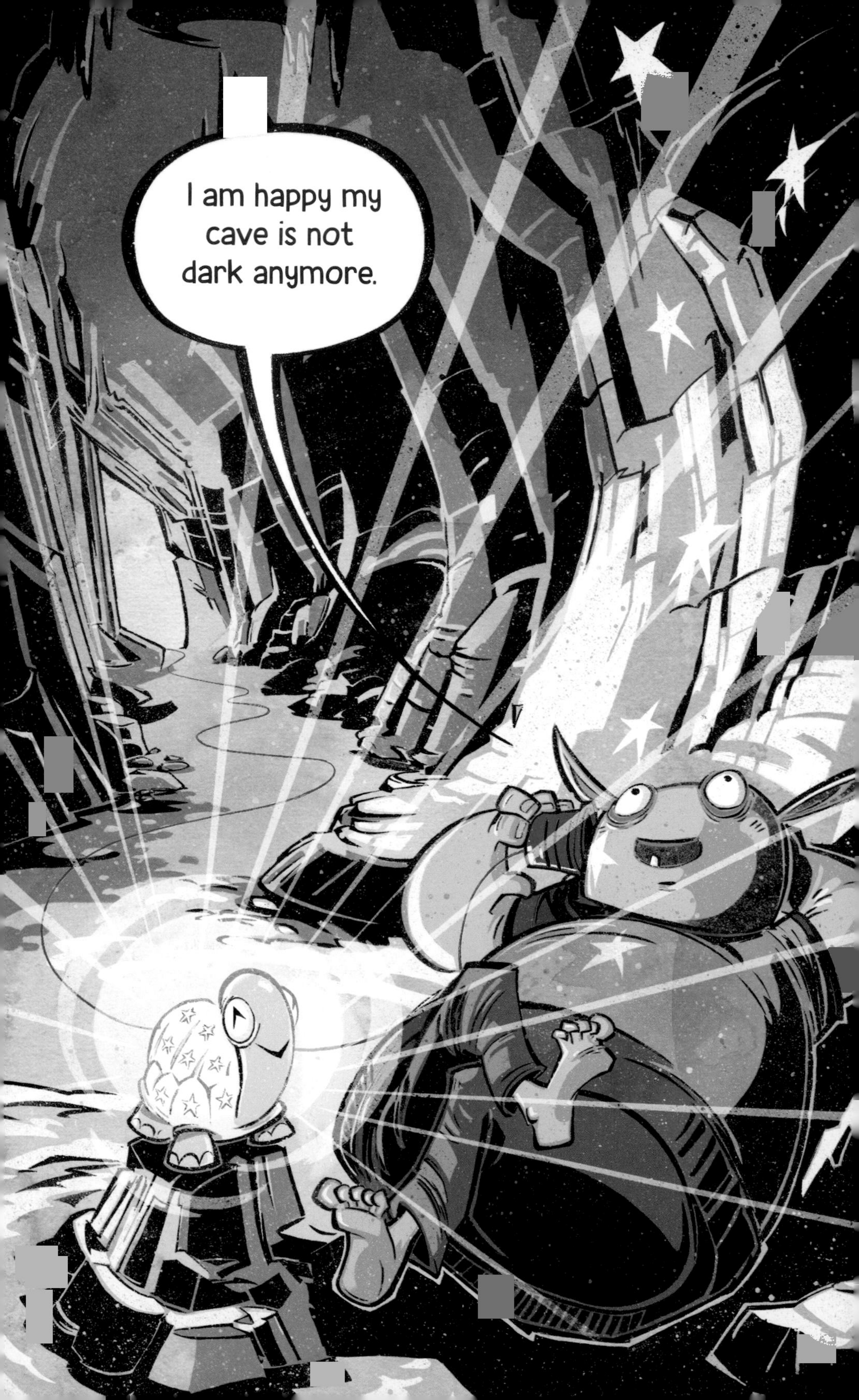
I am happy my cave is not dark anymore.

For my daughters, who can be so creative when they put down their phones.

I Like to Read® Comics instill confidence and the joy of reading in new readers. Created by award-winning artists as well as talented newcomers,these imaginative books support beginners' reading comprehension with extensive visual support.

We want to hear every new reader say, "I like to read comics!"

Visit our website for flash cards, activities, and more about the series:
www.holidayhouse.com/ILiketoRead
#ILTR

Printed and bound in May 2022 at C&C Offset, Shenzhen, China.
The artwork was created digitally on an iPad with Procreate.
www.holidayhouse.com
First Edition
1 3 5 7 9 10 8 6 4 2

Library of Congress Cataloging-in-Publication Data is available.

ISBN: 978-0-8234-5018-3 (hardcover)

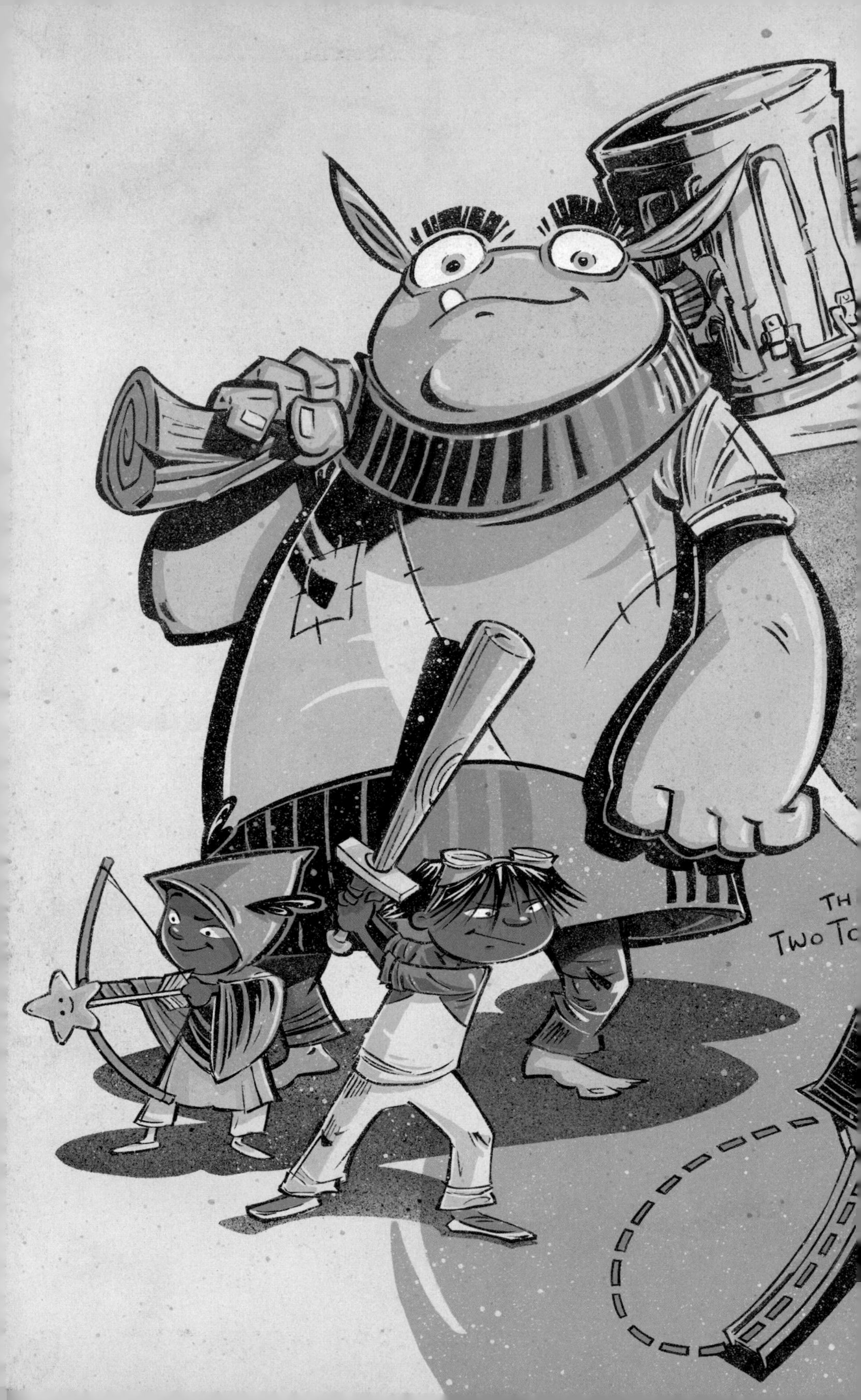
TH
TWO T